# LITTLE NIGHTMARES™

# THE LONELY ONES

E. C. MYERS

SCHOLASTIC INC.

ISBN 978-1-338-88895-9

10 9 8 7 6 5 4 3 2 1 25 26 27 28 29

Printed in the U.S.A. 40

First printing 2025

Book design by Martha Maynard

Bandai Namco Europe - Little Nightmares Team
Alizée Debart, Transmedia Manager
Lonnie Nadler, Franchise Narrative Director

# CHAPTER 1

The girl jolts awake, coughing. Her throat burns.

She gasps, trying to catch her breath. The air is humid and smells of grease and hot metal and hidden spaces.

When her heart stops thudding in her aching chest and she's breathing evenly, she tries to look around. This place is dark, except for bands of dim light filtering in from above. The glowing beams catch floating dust. This isn't her room at home, though she can't quite picture what her room looks like. She struggles to recall anything about it, or where she lives.

*Where am I?*

She's lying on a hard floor, her drenched clothes heavy against her skin. She pushes herself upright, and wet hair plastered over her forehead drips stinging water into her eyes. She swipes an arm across her face to dry it, but her soaked shirtsleeve only makes it worse. The water has a sharp scent that tickles her nose. Her lips taste bitter.

The puddle around her drains between damp wooden slats. *Drip. Drip. Drip.* Water plinks soft and steady far below her.

She realizes she's squeezing something tightly in her left hand. She unfolds her fingers and finds a bronze pocket watch in her palm.

Moisture beads inside the glass. The hands are frozen, with the short hand at the one, the long one just past the five. She taps the watch with a finger and then presses it to her ear, listening closely for the ticking of its delicate movement.

Nothing. It's broken.

She blinks away tears, pushing her feelings down out of habit, though there's no one here to see or reprimand her for weakness. Someone must have given her this watch, though she doesn't remember who, or why it's important. She slips it into her pocket, wondering why it's so hard to think about her life before—

Panic grips her as another question bubbles up.

*Who am I?*

This thought above all else frightens her. She doesn't know her own name. She concentrates hard until "Ruse" pops into her head.

Whether this is her name or simply a word she's heard or read once, it feels right. She calms down. Until she suddenly hears a sound behind her. Someone crying.

Ruse jumps up and whirls around, peering into the

dark room. Sickly bars of light illuminate two other children lying nearby. Her instincts scream at her to keep her distance from them, but curiosity ultimately brings her closer. She wants to see if she knows them, but she soon realizes these kids are not from her neighborhood. They look like they're not even from her own *time*, more like people she's glimpsed in faded photographs.

The closest child is a girl, hunched over with her knees drawn to her chest. Her back shakes as she sobs softly. Ruse shuffles toward her and the girl turns in alarm, eyes wide. Her right hand goes to her throat, where her pale skin is rubbed raw and bruised. She holds her left hand out like a warning or a plea: *Stop.* Her dusty hair is short, cut unevenly like no one cared how it looked. She wears worn, rough fabric, scraps really, held together with rope. A short length of rope also dangles from around her neck, its ends frayed and unraveling.

Ruse doesn't know why, but she immediately pities the girl. She holds out her hands, open with the palms facing out to show she means no harm. The girl's breath comes quick and ragged, both desperate and fierce. They stare at each other for a long time until Ruse hears a weak moan from the other kid. The boy.

Curled up in a fetal position, he's gaunt, almost skeletal. His clothes are stiff and grimy, his skin streaked with dirt. A red kerchief hides his nose and mouth. When he sees Ruse, he slowly pulls himself to his feet. He sways and steps toward her unsteadily.

No wonder he's wearing a mask. He stinks. She backs away.

He pauses, brows knit with concern, and glances from Ruse to the other girl. The three of them consider one another warily.

"Feast," he says in a hollow whisper, bony hands clutching his concave stomach. The word almost sounds like a question, or a request.

Ruse hesitates before replying, "Ruse." She shrugs her shoulders slightly.

They turn their attention to the rope girl, still crouched on the floor. Her eyes dart back and forth. Her lips part and she makes a barely audible, rasping noise. *"Mim."* Then the girl ducks her head and stares down at her knees.

"How did we—" Ruse begins just as the room shudders and she nearly falls over. A deafening, uneven melody starts up, tentatively at first but building in speed and intensity.

Mim clamps her hands over her ears. Feast reaches a hand down to her. She hesitates, studying his face cautiously, before she takes it. He hoists her up. As soon as she is standing, she pushes him away and covers her ears again.

The room brightens, more light filtering in from between the planks of the wooden wall. Dark shapes intermittently block the spare light, faster and faster, creating a strobing effect that makes Ruse's eyes hurt. But she can make out more details now: They're in a narrow, circular room, a cracked, wooden pole marking the center. The floor thrums beneath her feet. She can feel the vibration in her bones.

On the far end of the room, a large motor drives massive gears and a pulley turns a series of wheels. Above them, near the ceiling, a ring the size of the room is turning, picking up speed. Great billows of white steam hiss into the space. It's getting hotter. Ruse wipes sweat from her eyes. They are inside some vast machine.

The loud music sounds wrong, like an old, out-of-tune organ with missing pipes. Still, the discordant melody jars memories in Ruse's mind. She sees an ice-cream truck driving slowly through her neighborhood, luring children out of their homes with grubby fists of coins. She remembers her parents taking her to an amusement park in the Hatefields when she was small, and they were less important and had time for her.

She touches the broken watch in her pocket. She swallows. Pushes away the resurfacing memories and regret. The sadness and fear.

Ruse inches toward the outer edge of the room. Wet footprints trail behind her, though her clothes are somehow dry already. The lights strobing through the slats of the curved wall make her dizzy and she stumbles forward. She presses her hands against the wall until she regains her balance. Large splinters dig into her palms. The sharp pain helps clear her head. *I must keep moving,* she thinks. *Find a way out.*

She edges around the room, brushing against the wall with her left shoulder until finally she comes to a separation, then a hinge and . . . a door!

The door is much too big. The long handle is high above her head. Ruse stretches up on the tips of her toes, but no matter how hard she strains, her hands can't reach it.

Ruse sizes up the others. Mim is shorter than Ruse

but has about the same build. She leans against the opposite wall, head bowed and eyes squinched shut. Feast stands in front of the machinery, studying and poking at the engine curiously. He is slight, much thinner than either girl. The way his skin hangs loose on his body, he probably hasn't eaten in ages. He seems a little taller than Ruse, though it may just be the way his wiry dark hair sticks straight up like a scrub brush.

"Here!" Ruse calls out. She can't hear her own voice above the din of clashing notes, clanging machinery, and hissing steam, but Feast startles and turns, looking for her. She waves at him and then points up at the handle of the door. He heads toward her. Mim watches them silently.

The boy reaches up for the handle the way Ruse did, but it's out of his reach too. He jumps for it a few times and his fingertips just brush against it before he crashes back down. He shakes his head.

Feast crouches and beckons for Ruse to join him,

then pats his shoulders. He wants her to climb on him so she can reach the handle. But once the door is open, he could run out on his own and leave her inside. She's always being left behind.

He seems disappointed that she doesn't cooperate. He appeals to Mim next, reaching a hand out toward her. Ruse thinks the other girl is too scared to help, so she's surprised when Mim takes halting steps toward Feast.

He holds himself steady as she climbs onto his back and then stands on his shoulders. He grabs her ankles securely, and Ruse sees her flinch at the contact. He carefully stands as she balances in place, one hand on top of his head, the other reaching for the handle.

She just manages to grab it, but when she pulls, it doesn't budge. She takes hold of it with both hands, but she's either too weak or too light to pull it down. Feast yanks on her legs, and the handle moves down slightly. Mim cries out and he trembles with the effort.

They have to be heavier.

Ruse reluctantly moves to Feast's side and wraps him in a bear hug. She holds her breath and pulls down, adding her weight to his and Mim's.

The handle dips.

*Click.*

The door opens a crack, and the three children tumble into a mess of elbows, knees, hard heads, and soft stomachs.

Ruse untangles herself from the others and peers around the edge of the door.

They are at the center of a large carousel. The circular platform around them is moving counterclockwise, parading carved wooden creatures past the door: A large, black beetle with a glossy shell bobs up and down on its pole. A wasp with delicately carved wings and a barbed stinger as long as Ruse herself zips by. A fly—fat, heavy, and hairy with red compound eyes. A squat brown toad covered with bulbous warts and yellow spots.

Teetering on the backs of some of these crawlies are giant people with rotund bodies that remind Ruse of gobs of melting dough. Their heads have distorted, sagging features, folds of flesh indistinguishable from their shoulders. Their shirts strain to contain their bulging torsos, pasty skin showing between the buttons. They cling to their steeds with muscular arms and puffy thighs.

At first, she thinks they might be carvings as well, until one of the riders notices her and swivels its head to keep her in sight as it passes. Ruse quickly ducks back behind the door. Her heart pounds faster.

What Ruse feels is dread. Foreboding. It's the sense that she's going to regret this. She wants to listen to that tiny, sensible voice, but she also knows she can't stay here forever. Eventually the music will stop, the ride will stop, and these sad dough giants will discover her.

She scurries back into the motor room and lets the others check out what's on the other side of the door.

Feast looks out and studies the carousel, eyes narrowed in determination. Ruse figures this isn't the worst challenge she's ever faced.

Mim peers outside meekly and then backs away, trembling. She bumps into Ruse and recoils.

Feast comes back for them. He tugs gently at Mim's sleeve. She turns away.

Ruse tenses at the door. If she can sneak past the riders and get off the carousel, she'll be free to go wherever she likes. She's used to being on her own. Caring for others only results in suffering.

But her hands tremble. Her breath comes in quick, shallow gasps. She's quivery and weak all over. As if her body remembers something her mind doesn't. Hesitating on the precipice of doubt, fearing to take the plunge.

She shakes off these nagging feelings and takes deep breaths, steadying herself. Then, before she can question her choice, she charges across the threshold.

But she stumbles as soon as her right foot lands on

the rotating platform. She falls and sprawls out spread-eagle, clawing at planks with her fingers, digging in with her toes. The carousel is moving faster than it appeared. As she comes around, she glimpses Feast and Mim crouching inside the open door of the motor room. They watch her and, as she comes back around, Feast takes Mim's hand and drags her onto the platform with him.

He's smarter about it than Ruse and starts by running in the opposite direction the carousel is spinning. He pumps his legs to keep up and stay in place, and slowly makes progress, edging along until he reaches a stationary pole beneath a carved red ant with massive mandibles, thick as Ruse's arm and twice as long. He pulls Mim along with him and they wrap their arms around the pole.

Ruse surveys the spinning landscape once more. If Feast and Mim draw the attention of the giants riding the carousel, Ruse might have a better chance of slipping away. On the other hand, splitting up could increase the risk of one kid being spotted, which might spell danger for all three of them.

Ruse slowly climbs to a crouch, steadies herself on her hands and knees, and then darts forward, angling her approach toward the other kids. Feast holds on to the pole with his right hand and stretches his left out to her. He catches her by the arm and pulls her in close. He doesn't smell so bad outside, with the air rushing by them.

Out here, the music is not quite so earsplitting. They zoom past the source of the cacophony, a large organ at the center of the carousel. It has a gilded façade, the paint faded, pitted, and peeling, with an eye painted above the organ's pipes. Drums and cymbals are mounted on either side.

Ruse finds she has to focus on either Feast or Mim and try to tune out the background racing by or she can't keep her balance. Mim is peaked and sweaty like she's about to be sick.

*The carousel is going faster,* Ruse realizes. And more of the riders are noticing the kids huddled near the ant. They have to move soon.

Ruse points to a slimy, sluglike creature curled into a spiral. The mount's head is all mouth, gaping and dark.

Mim looks scared, but when Feast nods, his brow furrowed with concentration, the girl finds her strength. Ruse squeezes his hand and a moment later, he squeezes back.

Ruse grits her teeth and runs, the boy holding on to her left hand and staying just behind her. She grabs the next pole with her right hand and looks back. With their arms outstretched, they form a human chain connecting the two poles. Now Ruse holds on tight as Mim lets go of her pole and staggers forward, holding on to Feast as he and Ruse pull. The three of them cluster under the slug. As the creature rises and falls with the motion of the ride, its thick body hides them from view of the riders.

Ruse studies the next row of mounts and picks their next goal: a dun-colored moth with tattered wings. It's hideous, and she feels like if she gets too close, it might bite her—but she runs toward it anyway, tethered to her companions.

This time, she is startled when riders kick out at them as they race past. Their legs are short and thin, but one strikes a glancing blow to the side of Ruse's head. She stumbles and is briefly airborne, certain she will fly out and away from the others. But Feast doesn't let go.

Ruse's hand is slick with sweat. Her grasp begins to slip. Feast yanks hard and she gets her feet back under her. She adjusts her handhold, takes a moment to steady herself, and lunges for another pole.

Her fingers bump against it, but she can't grab on. Then suddenly, she lurches toward the pole and past it. The three of them are untethered from the ride. The violent momentum sends them head over heels toward the edge of the carousel.

Somehow Ruse manages to hold on to Feast's hand, and then abruptly he yanks her arm and she stops rolling and bouncing along the platform.

Her fingers locked with Feast's, Ruse looks back at her companions. Mim desperately hangs on to one of the countless red legs of a black centipede coiled around a nearby pole. Feast is caught between her and Ruse, straining to hold on to both of them. His breathing is ragged, his eyes squeezed against intense pain and focus. He's at his limit, and his grip is weakening.

Ruse twists around and looks above her—into the face of a rider perched on the back of a large, dun-colored moth.

The rider's face shows no recognition or reaction as he stares down at them. His placid eyes and expression are blank.

What does he want? What will he do if he catches them? And will he alert the others?

Ruse hopes she doesn't find out the answers to any of these questions.

*I have to get away from here*, she thinks. Then she feels the carousel stutter and slow. The music is slowing too. It will be easier for them to stay on their feet as the ride ends, but it will also be easier for the big people to catch them.

But she has an idea. They're close to the edge now, and they might make it if they run for it. They'll go faster if they go in the same direction the carousel is turning. Then as soon as the ride stops, they can scramble down to the ground before the big people can reach them. She waves at Feast and Mim with her free hand, and when they look at her, she points to her right, where she wants them to go.

The carousel continues to slow. The music plucks out harsh notes as it winds down.

*Thunk*. The floorboards creak and bounce as the rider clumsily dismounts from the moth, eyes still focused on the children. It holds on to a wing covered in cracked, peeling white paint, and tips toward them, swiping a pudgy hand at Ruse.

She lets go of Feast's hand and takes off, running clockwise along with the motion of the carousel. It takes her a few steps to get the pace of it, but then she is running, faster than she's ever run in her life. Almost too fast for her legs to keep up.

The platform shakes and she hears more thuds behind her. She risks a glance back and sees more of the big people hopping off their mounts and lumbering after Feast and Mim, running hand in hand behind Ruse. But the people are unsteady. Some of them topple and roll, tumbling over the side of the carousel or digging their fingers into the floor to keep from flying off.

Ruse keeps moving, angling outward toward the edge of the platform. The yellow bulbs illuminating the carousel are harsh enough that everything beyond is darkness, except for pinpricks of light that race by too fast and too disorienting to discern what's out there. Looking at them makes Ruse lightheaded and off-balance, so she focuses on the platform.

Even so, she feels the eyes of the riders tracking her as she passes them, and the heavy impact of their feet as they drop to the platform and pursue her. She has almost made a loop of the entire carousel, and ahead big people clumsily lurch and stumble toward her with grasping fingers and those vacant expressions.

The music clangs to a stop and the air rushing past her face becomes a gentle breeze. Beneath her feet, she feels the carousel shift into a lower gear. The ride grinds to a halt.

She keeps running straight for the platform's edge and uses her momentum to launch herself into the air.

Ruse hits the ground hard, tucks her legs in, and rolls. She spins and tumbles and finally skids to a stop, settling onto her back with the wind knocked out of her. She gasps there until she is able to breathe again.

She examines her arms and legs. Bruises and scrapes, but nothing is broken. Close by, Feast stands shakily. Though his slight frame droops with fatigue, he helps Mim onto her feet. A Giant Wheel looms on the horizon beyond them, mesmerizing as it spins lazily and red lights flash along eight concentric rings.

Heavy stomping snaps Ruse out of a trancelike state. She jumps up and glances back at the carousel, steeled to run from the big people. But they are moving away from the kids now, herding like cattle toward a cluster of tall striped tents and wooden carts.

On the carousel, the dough giants had been so intent on pursuing the children, with their odd, expressionless faces. Now they are docile, clearly fixated on some new distraction.

*Maybe they wanted to* play *with us?* Ruse wonders.

The thought makes her shudder. No matter their intentions, she imagines how roughly the giants would have handled her if she had been captured. Right now, the safest place seems to be wherever they aren't, so Ruse starts walking in the opposite direction from them. Strings of yellow fairy lights dangle overhead against the twilight sky, and Ruse catches faint strains of music from another attraction in the distance.

"Hey!" Feast calls out. Ruse stops and looks over her shoulder.

The boy rubs his left forearm nervously, his eyes hopeful. "Shouldn't we stay together?" he says.

Ruse glances between him and Mim. The other girl sighs and wraps her arms around herself. It was a good thing she hadn't withdrawn like that back on the carousel. If she had, none of them would have made it.

Ruse knows she also wouldn't even have made it this far without Feast and Mim. She doesn't know how the three of them came to this place, but they had needed to work together to escape the motor room and the carousel. Should she stick with them or find her own path from here on?

Teaming up seems like a reasonable strategy to survive, though Ruse would have no problem being alone. After all, she is certain they will leave her eventually—everyone always does. It might be smart to have company for once. So maybe they can keep helping one another. At least until they know more about where they are and why.

Ruse shrugs. She continues walking, eyes focused on a row of tattered tents flapping in the breeze. It's up to the others if they want to come along.

Feast and Mim fall into step with Ruse, and together they head down a path dimly illuminated by flickering orange bulbs.

# CHAPTER 2

The path leads the trio between rows of worn, empty caravans with cracked and missing wheels. Their rotten walls are falling apart, paint faded to the color of storm clouds. Ruse catches Feast looking wistfully behind them more than once, at the bright lights at the center of the carnival, twisty towers curving inward, a red-and-white-striped big top, the hypnotic Giant Wheel.

The breeze carries snatches of calliope music. Indistinct voices far away. The rumbling of a train or roller coaster. Wood creaks and groans around them, the way her house sounded on windy nights when Ruse lay awake in bed, frightened and alone.

Their steps echo hollowly on floorboards beneath their feet just like the ones in the carousel, even though they're outside now, and the ground itself seems to shift and tilt so that Ruse constantly feels like she's on uneven footing. Sometimes she imagines they are walking up a slight incline, then everything changes and it's more like going downhill.

The wind suddenly picks up, and a swaying tent ahead of them teeters and then collapses across their path with a *crash*. Ruse startles and Mim gasps as the strings of bulbs above flare brightly before they go out, leaving the path darker than before.

In the crepuscular natural light of this sunless place, Ruse makes out the hulking shape of the fallen tent. It has pulled the fairy lights down to the ground, their bulbs broken and crackling with blue lightning. Mim approaches one of the exposed light sockets with an outstretched hand until Feast pulls her back and shakes his head. Has she never seen a light bulb or electricity before? Has she no sense? She's no better than the neighborhood kids who followed . . .

Ruse shoves those thoughts away. While those kids back home might not have known what they were doing, Ruse certainly had, or thought she had.

And what does that say about *her*?

*Not now*, Ruse thinks. She carefully picks her way past shards of broken glass and buzzing sockets, following the broken lights to the tent.

The damaged wire is tangled up in torn fabric, popping and spewing blue-white sparks. The electric flashes cast long shadows on the ground. She smells smoke and an orange glow appears beneath the tent.

Feast waves her over and points to a brown hedge running parallel to their path. The top of the tent has crushed a section of the hedge. She nods and they head for it.

The hedge is as tall as the giants back at the carousel, too high for Ruse to see over it. But the tent has created a way through to the other side.

Mim tentatively plucks a leaf from the hedge with short, grubby fingers. She sniffs it curiously, frowns, and then passes it to Ruse.

Ruse runs her fingers over the foliage. It's dry and thin, like tissue. *Paper*, she realizes. But if it was never a living plant, how has it gone brown? She tears the "leaf" in half and lets the pieces slip between her fingers and drop to the ground.

Feast pushes his hands into the hedge and grabs fistfuls of paper. He tosses them over his head and the pieces drift around them like confetti until the air catches the papers and whips them away.

Ruse clambers onto the tent and scurries across the rough fabric. She reaches the end of it and drops down to the ground. Grass crunches under her feet. She stoops to touch the turf and finds it scratchy and unpleasant.

The others follow her and begin to look around. They are now between two hedge walls, which gives Ruse the impression of being both inside and outside. Combined with the peculiar sensation she's had that she is both high up and down low, Ruse is completely disoriented, like she's simultaneously here and nowhere at all.

*I'm here*, she thinks, forcing herself to focus on the moment instead of what came before. Nothing else matters now except finding a place where she doesn't feel confused or alone or invisible. Where she feels safe, if such a thing is possible.

She can sort of guess at what happened to Feast and Mim, but those stories were theirs to tell. Or not tell. Whatever had brought them here and brought them together, happy or sad—it wasn't an ending. It was a beginning.

Ruse marches between the hedge walls until the path turns to the right. As she continues on, the hedge on her left rustles. From the wind, or something inside it?

She walks faster, pausing only at another junction with three paths: straight ahead, left, and right. Feast and Mim stop behind her. When they stop moving, the rustling also stops.

Two thoughts occur to Ruse at the same time. *This is a maze*, and *Something's following us*.

Mim whimpers. Ruse checks on her: The girl is turning her head back and forth frantically. Feast tries to calm her down, though he seems perplexed about what's agitating her. He glances at Ruse, his eyebrows raised in a question. Ruse taps a finger to her right ear.

He tilts his head and listens, but the only sound is Mim's rapid breathing and the wind whistling outside the hedge maze. Ruse gestures for them to keep moving, then taps her ear again. She chooses the left path and creeps along it slowly to quiet her footsteps.

One . . . two . . . three . . . four . . . As she takes her fifth step, the hedge again stirs. It sounds like shuffling paper. She twists around to look behind them.

Feast is now on the alert, looking for the source, while Mim is wild-eyed and trembling. In the hedge wall behind them, Ruse sees two red eyes glowing behind brown leaves.

Ruse points, but by the time they look that way, the eyes are gone. Feast holds out his hands with his palms upturned. Ruse doesn't answer his unspoken question. She turn and runs.

The grass muffles the pounding of her feet on the curiously hollow ground, but whatever's inside the hedge is no longer sneaking. The maze explodes with noise. The thing rushes past Ruse inside the hedge wall on her right in a hurricane of skittering footsteps. The hedge shakes and paper leaves flutter out into the corridor, pelting Ruse as she keeps running. A sour, earthy smell fills her nostrils as she breathes.

The thing (or things?) is ahead of her now, but Ruse sees a new path off to her left and darts down it. She takes another path at random, then another. Each time she encounters a branch in the path, she takes whichever one leads away from the skittering and rustling paper. She's heading deeper into the maze, though she has no hope now of retracing her steps back to where they entered.

She keeps running.

The paths are getting narrower, the hedge walls rising higher and curving in over her head, so she can only see a sliver of dim sky.

Then she takes one more turn and ends up in a long, shadowed corridor. She slows to listen. She no longer hears too many feet scurrying in the hedge, only two pairs, Feast's and Mim's, as they catch up with her, gasping. Despite his obvious weariness, Feast's eyes are bright and piercing as he gazes at Ruse. She looks away uneasily.

Ruse advances cautiously. This path stretches on and on, longer than any of the others. Until she sees a wall ahead. Not a hedge wall, but a red brick one that stretches up and beyond the hedges. A dead end.

Too late, she realizes that the thing may have steered her here. But if so, where is it? As much as she dislikes the sound of it chasing her through the hedge, it's almost worse *not* hearing it now, when she is certain it's somewhere waiting.

Maybe if she hurries, she can make it back to the entrance of this corridor before it arrives. She is about to convey this plan to Feast and Mim, but they aren't beside her anymore. Panic stabs at her as she looks for them.

*There.* Feast and Mim are near the hedge on her right, tugging at something sticking out of the leaves near the ground. It takes the two of them, pulling and grunting, to finally yank it out into the corridor. They stumble backward and the object clangs to the ground: It's a pair of closed garden shears with dull rusted blades, a little taller than they are.

Feast studies the shears for a moment before he grabs one of the long metal handles. He looks expectantly at

Mim. She hesitates but takes the other handle. They pull on their halves of the tool, going in opposite directions. The blades stick a bit, but they creak open. Then Feast and Mim push the handles together and the blades snap closed. *SHIKT!* They try again and they move more smoothly. *SHIKT! SHIKT!*

Ruse hurries over to them and gestures at the small break in the leaves where the clippers came from. She mimics the scissors with two fingers. Feast's eyes shine a bit and she imagines him smiling as he whispers something to Mim. She looks doubtful, but together they jab open the shears and jab them back into the hedge opening. Feast and Mim coordinate their actions to close the shears and cut into the brown foliage.

*SHIKT!*

Feast makes an approving murmur and they continue cutting away at the hedge. Paper leaves and cut branches tumble out. Ruse wonders how long it will take them to cut through to the other side and what they will find there, but then she hears that rustling from before and a louder, faster slicing sound. *TCH TCH TCH*. She calls out a warning and looks down the corridor as paper leaves burst out of a hedge and something crawls out.

She sees its flattened head first: waving antennae, red eyes, snapping fangs. It takes some time for its body to emerge completely, segment by segment. Fifteen in all, and each armored with a dark plate and sprouting long, barbed legs that carry it forward with a wavelike motion.

It's as if the Centipede on the carousel has been brought to life.

It hisses and scurries toward them, frightfully fast. Ruse backs up and bumps into Feast. There's nowhere they can go unless . . .

Feast and Mim's work with the shears has expanded the hole in the hedge enough for them to crawl into it one at a time.

Ruse pushes and squeezes her way through the brambly opening. When she emerges on the other end, she's surprised to find herself in a cavernous room. The hedge is hollow! Dim light filters through walls of fake leaves, dappling the floor.

Ruse turns and instinctively grabs Mim's cold hands to help her inside, dropping them as soon as the other girl is clear. Next, Feast shoves the shears through, handles first, and Ruse takes them. He scrambles through himself just before the Centipede arrives outside. Ruse spies it through the opening, feeling about with its long, wavy antennae. It is crawling around, making an ever-widening circle. A second set of long appendages at the back that resemble its forward antennae sweep back and forth along the ground. Searching.

Despite its bulbous red eyes, it seems to be blind. Which means it must be locating them by sound.

Ruse puts a finger over her lips and steps lightly and slowly, heading through the hedge toward the start of the corridor. She notes large, translucent fragments scattered inside the hedge, their edges rough as though something has gnawed at them. Eggshells? Some sections are more intact, reminding her of the Centipede's segments, with transparent, hollow legs still attached.

Some crawlies shed their skin like a snake. She used to find brittle pieces of them in Nanny's garden, beside the swimming pool. She shudders.

This is where it lives.

*CRUNCH.* Ruse swivels her head toward the sound and sees Mim standing on crushed bits of shell.

Suddenly the floor trembles, vibrating like there are dozens of feet pounding on it.

She hears scurrying behind her and turns just as the Centipede's fangs cut through the hedge wall—*TCH TCH TCH!*—and it barrels inside the hedge. It skitters and twists around, knocking Feast and Mim down. The shears clatter to the ground near them.

The Centipede lunges for Ruse. She dodges and rolls

away, its fangs snapping closed where she had just been standing.

Mim makes a choking sound. Ruse pulls herself up and sees the Centipede rearing up over her now, hissing and waving its antennae. Its fangs clack and its long front legs whip toward Mim. One of them wraps around her and drags her away.

But Feast grabs the shears and swings them hard against the leg, detaching the limb from its body. Mim pulls herself from its grip and scrambles away backward to the wall of the hedge.

"Don't move," Ruse whispers. The Centipede wheels toward her and lashes its legs, slapping the floor in front of her with a thud. Ruse blinks in reaction to the movement but somehow holds her body completely still. Her nostrils burn from its acrid stench, and she wrinkles her nose, trying not to sneeze.

It advances slowly and inquisitively in her direction, eyes burning red. *It doesn't see me*, she thinks. She hopes.

An antenna brushes the floor a foot in front of her. Then Ruse hears a scraping sound from the far side of the space. Quick as a thought, the Centipede whirls away, focused on its new prey, which happens to be Feast, dragging the heavy shears along the ground.

*What's he doing?* Ruse wonders.

Feast holds the shears up in front of him as the Centipede poises to attack. It pounces on him and the shears strike a glancing blow on its hard underside. *CRACK!*

The force knocks Feast to one side and the tool to the other, between him and Ruse. The Centipede shakes its head. Dark fluid drips from a small gash in its third segment. It moves in on Feast again, but a knocking sound to Ruse's left distracts it.

Mim.

She's trying to divert its attention away from Feast. And it's working.

Ruse uses the opportunity to run for the shears,

again drawing the Centipede's attention. It doesn't know where to attack next. It swivels its head and moves its body in a circle, hissing. The air grows thick with its chemical, earthy scent. Ruse nearly gags.

Feast picks himself up and heads for the shears too. Ruse gets there at the same time he does and they each grab one handle. As they struggle over the shears, pulling them back and forth, the blades open and close.

Mim runs toward them, the Centipede in close pursuit. Ruse and Feast lock eyes and pause with the shears open, no longer working against each other. And the moment that Mim passes them, Ruse and Feast slam the shears shut behind her, just in time to catch the Centipede between the sharp blades.

*SHIKT!*

The Centipede hisses and bucks as the shears slice between two of its segments and then break apart, leaving Ruse holding one handle and blade, her arms smarting from the impact.

The forward third of the Centipede lands hard and keeps scurrying. Slimy organs stretch behind it to the motionless section dragging along the floor.

Ruse and Feast drop the broken shears with a clatter, but the insect pays them no mind. It continues its slow, agonizing journey away from them, leaving a dark, wet trail.

Mim covers her eyes. Feast crouches on his hands and knees, head down. Ruse knows she would normally look away in disgust from such a gory sight, but she can't pry her eyes from it. She is fascinated by the Centipede's efforts to save itself. Even with its body broken and dying, it doesn't give up.

She marvels too that she and the others were able to defeat it. *We aren't helpless anymore*, she thinks. *We might survive. Together.*

She doesn't know why Feast had been willing to risk himself to fight the Centipede, but she's certain it's the first time anyone else has ever protected her from anything. At least, not for selfish reasons.

She watches the Centipede for a long while until it finally stops moving. Until Mim tugs on her shirt sleeve urgently and Ruse notices that the air is getting hazy.

Feast points and she sees light shining through the leafy wall of the hedge. Had someone fixed the fairy lights? But no, it's a harsher, orange glow. She smells smoke.

*Fire.*

Ruse remembers the tent, the live wire of the fallen lights, the first signs of fabric catching fire. The tent had collapsed onto the paper hedge.

They have to get out of here.

They can't cut themselves a new exit now, with the shears ruined. Feast grabs Ruse's hand and pulls her back toward the hole in the hedge wall. But that will only lead them back into the maze while it burns around them. She follows along while her mind races. She looks back at the Centipede again. It had crawled all the way to the brick wall at the end of the hedge maze. Why? It wasn't just trying to get away from her and the others, it had been going somewhere. It was trying to get to safety, just like them.

Ruse yanks her hand free and hurries over to the Centipede. While Feast and Mim hang back fearfully, she stands in front of its head and turns to face the direction it had been headed: toward the wall. She runs straight ahead and examines the wall, looking for any crack or weakness.

It's Feast that spots the gap when he and Mim join her to see what she's doing. He kneels and indicates a section of missing mortar between one of the bottom bricks and the ground, which has been worked away a bit. Ruse is surprised that the Centipede could have squeezed through, when the opening looks almost too narrow for even her.

Feast lowers himself inside first, climbing backward. He holds on to the edge for a moment, knuckles white, before he drops. Ruse hears a soft *WHUMP* below.

Ruse peers down. Feast's pale face glimmers in the sliver of weak light from the opening.

"It's not far," he calls out.

Ruse sits and slides her feet and legs through the crevice. Her heart races with anticipation and nervousness. She hesitates.

*Jump*, she hears, but she isn't sure whether it's her own inner voice or Feast encouraging her or an echo of memory.

Ruse jumps.

*WHUMP.* Her feet hit a wooden floor almost instantly. The abrupt landing unbalances her, and Feast reaches out to steady her. But that small effort causes him to topple against her, so she has to hold *him* up. He leans heavily on her arm for a moment. Then he steps away and gestures for her to help Mim instead.

Ruse turns and catches the girl as she slips down to join them.

When Ruse stretches her arms out at her sides, her fingertips just brush rough, dirt-packed walls. She reaches up and her hand touches a wooden ceiling just over her head. *It's such a narrow space.* Her breath quickens.

Feast beckons. Ruse squints to see what lies ahead of them, but darkness is all there is. He takes her right hand reassuringly and whispers, "I'll be our eyes."

*Can he really see in the dark?* Even if he can, Ruse considers whether she is willing to follow, completely dependent on his senses and good sense. The last time she had trusted someone completely, hardly a stranger, she had paid a terrible price. Feast squeezes her hand, and after a moment, she squeezes back. She reaches behind her, and Mim takes her left hand. It's like holding on to a cold, limp flower. The three of them are linked again. Ruse wonders what other ties may be binding them together here.

Feast shuffles forward, guiding them into the black beyond.

# CHAPTER 3

**Ruse trudges along between Feast and Mim** in the blind crawl space for what seems like hours, but what is more likely mere minutes. Does time actually exist in such darkness? Even if she could check her watch—she can't even see her own hand holding Feast's—it's stuck at the moment she left everything she knew and entered this place.

The solidity, the weight of the watch in her pocket, is nonetheless comforting. A piece of home, a reminder of where she came from. Of what she's left. She is startled to realize she has no desire to return there.

Without anything to look at, her thoughts turn inward. Scenes from her old life flash before her eyes, more impressions than memories. Her imagination fills in the blank moments, confusing what was with what should have been.

Against the darkness she sees a fine home filled with everything a child should like—but perhaps not all that one needed. She may not be able to recall details, but she remembers how she had often felt: the intensity of *wanting* . . . Companionship. Attention. Parents who didn't think caring meant buying her more things.

Ruse can't picture her mother or father at all anymore. But she can't forget Nanny. The gentle old woman had loved every child in their neighborhood, maybe too much.

Mim squeaks and Ruse's past fades back into the darkness. Something brushes against her legs in the tight space. Her heart flutters in her chest. As it continues on past Feast, she hears his dry voice croak, "Pardon."

Ruse shudders. *What is that?* Even as she completes the thought, another one of the creatures shoves by. Then another, and another. She hears a squealing chorus behind her and she glances back. Somehow there is now enough light for her to make out a roiling mass of bodies with greasy, matted fur and whipping tails.

Rats!

The large rodents clamber around the kids. The children press against a wall to let them go by.

The creatures smell of popcorn, musk . . . and smoke. The crawl space is gradually brightening with sickly orange light from the way they came. The scorched air tickles Ruse's throat and her eyes water.

Ruse coughs. *The hedge maze is on fire*, she thinks. Will the building they're in burn too?

The last of the rats scamper ahead, their scratching claws and squeaks rapidly receding. The encounter has left Ruse even more uneasy, knowing there are other things moving down here with them. Small creatures and maybe bigger ones. Harmless things and hidden dangers.

Ruse and the others hurry deeper into the building, away from the light and smoke. The fiery glow gradually fades and Ruse can breathe more easily. But she can still see the shapes of Feast and Mim. There's more light ahead.

Hazy yellow beams slant down between the floorboards of rooms several feet above them. They pass large objects littering the dirty floor of the crawl space: a bent needle, snippets of thread, a black button. She hears a familiar sound nearby: the soft crackle and hiss of a needle on a record when the song has run out.

The sound grows louder as they keep moving, until she is below a floor vent. Ruse stops and peers through the holes. She sees the corner of a gramophone with a brass horn that plays nothing but silence as a platter spins on its turntable. She detects motion from the corner of her eye.

Someone big is inside the room, but all she can glimpse are oversized hands in white gloves coming in and out of her narrow view. It is gesturing quietly in front of a mirrored wall. Its thin arms and light, wrinkled skin are unlike the massive dough people enjoying the carnival outside.

Ruse can't take her eyes off the silent Performer. She has to see more.

Someone takes her hand and Ruse blinks. She is startled by a giant eye watching *her* through the holes in the vent. She opens her mouth to scream, but she makes no sound. And still she cannot look away.

Shadow surrounds the white eye, a shining light at the end of a tunnel. At its center, pinpricks of black and red.

A hand squeezes hers. Slowly, Ruse becomes more aware of her surroundings. Feast is tugging at her hand, trying to get her to move. Nearby, Mim holds her hands over her ears, her eyes tracking the giant figure in the room above them.

Ruse flits her eyes back to the floor vent, but the eye is gone. A foot in a brown slipper and black socks moves out of view, and a moment later, a door creaks open and closes with a soft click.

Mournful piano music seeps from the speaker of the record, mid-song. The gentle melody is familiar: a slower rendition of the calliope song that had blared from the carousel.

Ruse numbly follows Feast through the crawl space. The piano chords fade as they leave the Performer's room behind. But without the music, Ruse detects soft footfalls on the floors above, creaky doors swinging open and closing around them. Someone is moving about up there, searching.

She keeps her head down, focusing on her feet and the rat tracks in the dirt before them. She's afraid that if she looks up, she will see or be seen by the Performer again. Where the mindless attention of the dough giants had seemed akin to moths drawn to a flame, his had been keener, full of curiosity and intent.

Feast pauses each time they hear the footsteps, until another door opens elsewhere in the building. Sometimes near them, sometimes farther. How is the Performer covering so much distance so quickly? Feast leads them away from the sounds, and once again Ruse has the idea that they are somehow being directed in this underground labyrinth, just like in the maze. Then Ruse hears indistinct carnival music. They must be close to an exit! Excitedly, Ruse rushes ahead past Feast. His soft protest gives her a twinge of regret, but she is choosing her own way again. She won't be led anymore or trapped down here. She won't be hunted any longer.

And then she finds their way out of the crawl space. The floorboards of one room have caved under the weight of a dusty brown trunk. Its lid is just beneath the jagged hole in the splintered wood. If they could climb up there, they could easily walk up one of the broken boards and out. But it's too high for them to reach, even on one another's shoulders.

Ruse, Feast, and Mim consider the trunk and one another, trying to think of a way up. Mim nervously fiddles with the frayed ends of the rope dangling from her neck. If they had a longer rope and could get one end of it up there . . .

That's it! Ruse points to Mim's rope. The girl drops her hand self-consciously and turns away. She doesn't understand, and neither does Feast. Ruse opens her mouth to explain, but the distant sound of a door opening and closing makes her hold her tongue. She holds up her hands, gesturing for them to wait. Then she turns and races back down the crawl space the way they had come.

"Hey!" Feast whispers. Immediately, Ruse hears a door slam somewhere and open much closer. Then urgent footsteps resuming their search. She runs faster.

*I know I saw it somewhere*, she thinks. She follows the broken dirt along the path they had tread, all the way back to the Performer's room. The music is no longer playing, the needle bumping at the end of the record, regular as a heartbeat. *Ba-dum. Ba-dum. Ba-dum.*

She finds what she's looking for. A long white thread. She coils the string and loops it through an arm and over her shoulder. She'll need an anchor. As she tries to choose between a bent needle and a glossy button the color of midnight, she realizes the thumping record player has fallen silent. She listens hard, but she can't hear anything, even her own heartbeat.

Suddenly, the crawl space is awash with light as the floor above her lifts away soundlessly—a trapdoor she hadn't noticed before. She registers a blur of soft black shoes, wrinkled ankles, a flash of white. She quickly snatches the silver needle from the ground and jabs it upward. It sinks deep into the palm of a gloved hand

and is pulled away from her as it flinches. She feels the silent rage of the Performer but she avoids looking at his face. She grabs the black button, hoists it over her head like a shield, and runs. The door slams shut behind her and she hears a series of other doors opening and closing behind her in rapid succession, gradually becoming more and more distant. She hasn't much time before he catches up and finds her.

Panting, she reaches the room with the broken floor. The others aren't there, but she dares not call out. Had the Performer gotten to them too?

She's relieved when first Feast and then Mim slowly emerge from behind the fallen trunk. Feast's eyes glimmer when he sees what she's brought. But his brow furrows in concern as he notes the state she's in. She places a finger over her mouth to keep him from asking, and instead he helps her tie the thread through the buttonholes.

Feast points to a leather handle near the top of the

trunk. Ruse nods and starts swinging the button at the end of the thread to build up momentum. With a final swing, she plays out the thread and the button arcs up toward the handle. It glances off it and tumbles back to the ground with a *thunk*.

A door creaks nearby. They freeze as soft footsteps shuffle around for a moment. Then the door closes.

Low music drifts down from the room above. Ruse can't quite make sense of the jarring composition yet, so she concentrates on one instrument at a time. Her focus shifts from flute to piano, piano to mandolin, mandolin to accordion. Some sounds she can't identify at all.

Feast untangles the string and tries a different approach, hurling the button at the handle like a discus thrower. Lacking strength, his toss sends it well short of the mark. Ruse winces as it hollowly hits the side of the trunk and falls back down.

A door softly opens, and they wait with bated breath. It closes gently.

Feast is about to try again, when Mim steps forward and surprises her by reaching for the button. Ruse smiles and hands it over.

Mim carefully weighs the button and squints up at the handle of the trunk thoughtfully. She lets the button dangle from the string for a while, swinging like a pendulum. It gradually swings higher and she lets out more string, and then when it reaches the height of its arc, it flies gracefully through the air and over the handle, looping around once and barely making a sound. She pulls the thread taut and it twangs softly.

Feast pats Mim on the back. Mim smiles shyly and ducks her head.

Ruse nods and then starts climbing to the trunk's handle. From there she is able to hoist herself up to the top of the chest, where the leather is worn and cracked. Something dark is smeared along the surface like old paint, long dried and flaking. A large fresh handprint is outlined in the dust covering the lid. Ruse suppresses a sneeze and looks over the edge, down at Feast and Mim below. She waves them up.

Mim climbs next. When she reaches the leather handle, she waits for Feast to follow her up the thread. Ruse helps pull them to the top of the trunk. Then they turn to the broken board resting along it, which serves as a ramp to the floor above. They walk side by side, up and into the room.

# CHAPTER 4

The room is lit with bare light bulbs suspended from the rafters. All around are tall wood shelves crammed full of assorted objects. One column holds different kinds of lights, from floor lamps to lanterns. Another holds a variety of chairs and stools. A third is dedicated to dishes, tea sets, and silverware.

A cone-shaped speaker on a wall crackles with low, grating music, what it might sound like if every instrument was playing a different part of a song, or different songs entirely. The unsettling noise makes it difficult to think.

The speaker sits above a wooden door marked BACKSTAGE, which is secured with a rusted metal padlock. If the door is locked from the inside, there must be another way in and out of this room. Or perhaps a key.

Ruse strays from the others to search. She studies a shelf holding a long row of books with incomprehensible titles and cloth binding in a rainbow of colors. She tugs one off the shelf. It's almost as tall as her, but surprisingly light. She lowers it to the floor and opens the cover. The first page is blank.

Ruse flips through the rest of the pages. Every one of them is empty. She checks another book: same thing.

She scans the other shelves. Black apples? She reaches into a crate and pulls one out, almost dropping it because it is so light. She taps a finger against the dull surface and it sounds hollow inside. It's been carved from wood. But why paint it the wrong color?

She looks over at Feast just as he plunges a short dagger into his stomach. She gasps and starts toward him, but stops when he pulls the dagger out and winks. He's unharmed. He pushes a finger against the blade tip and it retracts, then springs back into place.

Mim is pulling apart a bouquet, smelling the tulips and roses and daisies and then tossing them to the floor in disgust. Is anything real here?

*They're props*, Ruse realizes. Pretend versions of real things crafted from paper and fabric and wood, for films and shows and things. Fake, like the paper grass and hedges outside.

She passes a shelf loaded with a variety of masks in all colors, some whimsical and some spooky. She lifts a white one with a long bird's beak. The eyes are large and sunken, one round like a full moon, the other smaller, a sort of wink.

The mask is just Ruse's size. She starts to lift it to her face, but instead she carefully places it back on the shelf. She doesn't feel like playing anymore.

She turns away from the shelves and is startled to discover a yellow clapboard house at the other end of the room. It seems familiar.

Ruse slowly approaches it. Her heart flutters as more details come into sharper focus, like adjusting binoculars. Hasn't she seen that blue door before and the lantern hanging over it?

And the backyard pool.

It stretches before Ruse as if she could just step right over the edge and sink into the cool water. Its placid surface reflects an inky sky. Stars seem to float on it or deep within. Other things float there too. She smells chlorine and nightshade.

A figure lurks in the shadows and beckons Ruse forward. The lantern light flickers.

Ruse only wants to be somewhere safe. She dips a

toe into the water and watches ripples spread across the pool, scattering stars and bodies. She tenses her muscles, preparing to—

*Jump!*

Ruse starts forward, but something yanks her back.

Feast pulls her away from the pool. She struggles from his grip and tries to go back to it. But now she no longer sees a pool there, only the image of a decaying yellow house on a canvas backdrop for a theatrical production. The painted fabric hangs from a sagging frame, situated against a wall between two columns of shelves. Empty paint cans are scattered on the floor beneath it, one of them on its side and spilling a dark, viscous liquid. A paintbrush juts out from another can that smells like turpentine.

Ruse looks down. Her foot is wet—with paint, not water.

She rubs her eyes. "Thank you," she whispers to

Feast. The discordant music nearly drowns out her voice, and she can't even be sure she spoke the words aloud. Her head is all jumbled from the noise and whatever she thought she had seen and felt.

Feast nods and then looks around urgently. He rushes to the end of the shelves and around a corner. Ruse hurries after him. It now seems like a bad idea to split up.

They find Mim shivering with her arms around herself as she stares at another painted backdrop. The scenery shows a cobblestone street flooded with mud and waste. Sheet-wrapped bundles are stacked like firewood in front of a dilapidated farmhouse. It looks like it might have been a nice place to live once.

Feast leans down and whispers something in Mim's ear. A moment later, she stands and turns her back to the painting.

"Do you know that place?" Ruse asks softly.

Mim shrugs. Then she shakes her head and walks past Ruse. Feast trails after her.

Ruse is curious about whether Mim saw something too. Did Feast? She's curious about what brought the three of them together and why. But she understands that they might not want to talk about it . . . or can't.

Each time Ruse almost remembers something about her life before, the memory slips away. All she recalls is how those lost moments make her feel.

Lonely.

From another aisle, Feast calls, "Here!"

Ruse races past more shelves and stage scenery until she sees him pointing at a door with black-and-white vertical bands. Pressure throbs behind her eyes, the stripes blurring and blending and difficult to concentrate on for long. An ornate silver handle is on its left side. If she climbs the shelves nearby, she should be able to leap and grab onto it.

The door looks odder the closer they get to it. It no longer appears to be a real, three-dimensional object, more like—

*Another picture!* Ruse presses her hands against the "door" and pushes. The paint is fresh, rough and tacky to the touch. It doesn't come off on her hands, but her palms itch and tingle.

She backs away, wiping her hands on her shirt until the strange sensation goes away.

Feast raps his knuckles on the painted wall. *Knock, knock, knock.* Mim backs up.

"Mim?" Ruse asks.

Mim covers her ears, gaze fixed on the wall.

Ruse listens at the wall beside the door, not wanting to touch the paint again. But she doesn't hear anything. That's when Ruse realizes with relief that the music has stopped. Her head already feels clearer.

"Check behind the scenery," she says. They scatter and peek behind backdrops. Ruse carefully avoids touching them. She is looking around a painting of an ocean when a door creaks open somewhere in the room. She ducks behind the canvas and cautiously peers out, trying to locate the others.

Feast is scaling up a column of shelves across from her. Suddenly, he glances over his shoulder and quickly climbs onto a shelf of small porcelain statues. He ducks behind them just as a tall figure passes by.

Ruse darts her eyes away. She only saw him long enough to register dark clothes and huge, white-gloved hands, which tell her it's the Performer they encountered earlier.

He steps softly through the room. Ruse dare not look at him directly, but she listens to him stop and rummage through props periodically. All the while, her eyes search out Mim. With no sign of her, she checks on Feast.

The boy is slowly creeping out from behind the statues. He turns his head back and forth, likely looking for her and Mim. Ruse risks waving her hand to get his attention, hoping the Performer doesn't glance her way. Feast notices her and raises his hand—and accidentally knocks one of the statues off the shelf.

Ruse winces in anticipation of the crash that will draw the Performer's attention immediately, but the sound never comes. She looks over in surprise and sees the broken shards of the figurine on the floor. A black mist distorts the air above it before quickly dissipating.

Feast has one hand over his masked mouth and is gesturing with the other, waving it forward as if saying, *Go back*. But he isn't looking at Ruse. She sneaks to the corner of a wood shelf and cautiously looks around it.

Mim stands in the center of the room, reaching in front of her as though she is picking up invisible objects from thin air. Out of the corner of her eye, Ruse sees the Performer making the same motions as he selects items from the shelves. He and Mim are moving in perfect sync.

While he faces away from her, Ruse soaks in more details about the Performer. He is tall enough to reach the highest shelves with thin, wrinkly arms. He wears a loose black vest over a long shirt with black-and-white stripes. A gray beret with thin black stripes caps his mop of curly brown hair.

He stoops and pulls black apples from a crate, tucking them into his vest. Ruse leans forward to watch. She counts six apples, but she can't see how he can be carrying them or any of the other items he has been taking. They just seem to disappear into invisible pockets.

He pauses and straightens. He lifts the beret from his head and places an apple under it, nestled in his coiled locks. When he lowers the beret, it covers the apple completely as though it isn't even there. Ruse can't help it—she claps.

Though her hands make no sound, the Performer

tilts his head toward her. She ducks back behind the shelf before she can see his face. Before he could see her, she hopes.

She leans against the wooden shelves and waits. A narrow shadow advances down the aisle toward her. She looks up as the fingers of a white hand grab hold of the side of the shelving unit. Her pulse races and she holds her breath.

She is surprised and relieved when the hand moves away and the Performer's shadow recedes. Then she hears a door creaking and a burst of static from the speaker on the wall. A hushed, distorted voice says, "Talent to the stage. The show is about to begin."

Feast clambers down from the shelves and hurries down the aisle, beckoning for Ruse to come with him. She pulls herself together and follows.

The Performer is gone. Mim is gone. Feast waits where the girl had been a moment ago, duplicating the Performer's actions. When Ruse catches up to him, he guides her back to the picture of the striped door on the wall. Only, it has changed: The door is slightly ajar.

Ruse tentatively touches it. It's solid now. She leans her head to the side, looking through the opening. It's dark and quiet on the other side. She signals to Feast to take a look with his better eyes, but his attention is elsewhere.

Feast looks down at something on the floor, caught in the door. He bends over and picks it up.

It's Mim's rope.

# CHAPTER 5

**Ruse can think of several reasons not to go** through the impossible door into the dark unknown, and only one reason why she has to.

Because Mim is on the other side.

Ruse is surprised and mildly annoyed to realize that she actually cares about the other girl. When did that happen? Ruse had been so ready to head off on her own, but whenever she left Mim and Feast, something always pulled her back . . .

Ruse reluctantly admits she doesn't prefer being

alone. But there's more to it. Whenever Mim and Feast had the chance to leave Ruse, they hadn't. They don't just need her help to survive: They *want* to be with her.

That's enough for her to follow Mim, and enough for Feast. They hold hands and step through the door.

They emerge in the shadows to the right of a stage, bare except for a wooden crate and chair at the center. The flooring is painted a matte black, dully reflecting lights mounted above in its glossy surface. The plaintive notes of a flute play over hidden speakers, the same song she has heard twice before.

Another painted backdrop is mounted at the back of the stage, this one depicting a cold gray room full of long tables. Hooks hang from the ceiling and metal drains are set into the floor. Dark stains spatter the walls and Ruse looks away from them quickly. She turns back to the door, but it is once again only a painting. They'll have to find another way out, after they find Mim.

Downstage on Ruse's right is a dusty black curtain.

She rushes across the slippery floor and lies on her stomach to peek through the curtain's frayed red tassels. In the audience, the stadium seats are filled with those misshapen giants from the carousel. Some of them clutch crumpled, greasy paper bags. They shovel handful after handful of chunky brown snacks into their mouths. Their chewing, crunching, and slurping makes Ruse feel queasy.

Like the stage, the crumbling walls of the cube-shaped theater are painted black from top to bottom. Up a sloping aisle and four shallow steps, open double doors lead out to a lobby. Ruse considers how they can get to them without being seen.

The music cuts off and the lights dim. Ruse and Feast scamper back to stage right. They push to the back of the wing, against the painted black-and-white door. Across from them, a tall man emerges from stage left. From high above the auditorium a spotlight shines down on him, making him the center of attention.

For the first time, Ruse sees the Performer's face. It's a luminous white, with dark, mismatched shapes around his eyes that make him look both surprised and sinister. Black paint is smeared in a sloppy, puckered smile. The striped beret perched in his corkscrew hair hangs low over one, flat ear, which is pale but unpainted like the rest of his wrinkled, sagging skin.

The Performer reaches his right hand forward, gloved fingers closed, and then slowly pulls it back as though it takes enormous effort. As he does so, he slides across the floor toward the center of the stage, feet at a sharp angle in front of him. Still holding on to what seems like nothing, he reaches his left hand forward and repeats the pulling motion. Again, he slowly slides forward.

For an instant, Ruse sees a blurry rope between his hands, stretched taut. She blinks, and it's gone. But he continues to pull himself along the stage with this invisible rope.

When he reaches the table in the middle, he releases his hands and promptly falls backward. He immediately bounces back up to his feet and turns to bow at the audience. His beret falls off.

He scoops it up, stands upright, and puts it back squarely on his head. Then he turns to walk toward the back of the stage and trips over the rope, tumbling over his feet and onto his back. Ruse laughs.

Feast taps her shoulder to get her attention. She shakes him off and keeps watching the Performer's antics. He has gotten himself all tangled up in the rope, his arms pinned down to his sides, and he bumbles around with his hands fluttering like a trapped bird.

Feast covers Ruse's eyes with a hand and she finally turns toward him in annoyance. He whispers something urgently, but she can't hear him. He touches his throat and frowns. He must be starving and may not last much longer without food, but does he want to eat *now*?

"What?" Ruse whispers—at least she means to. But her voice is gone too. The theater is completely silent.

The audience illuminated by the spotlight around the performer appears to be clapping and laughing uproariously, bits of food and spit flying from their open mouths—but Ruse doesn't hear anything.

She snaps her fingers, but still nothing. She breathes faster, her heart beats faster. But she can't hear any of it. Panic swirls inside her. From the uneasy look in Feast's eyes, he feels the same way. She jerks her head behind her, telling Feast they should go. But he shakes his head and looks back at the stage. He points to the crate.

The Performer, having freed himself from his imaginary bonds, acts like he's picking up the painted knife from the table in the backdrop. He brandishes his fist in front of him. She can almost see the shimmering serrated blade and curved black handle of a knife in his right hand. Then she notices that the knife in the painting is gone.

Ruse feels the vibration of the audience stomping their feet in appreciation, even though she can't hear anything.

The Performer cups his left hand around an ear, head tilted. Then he hides his right hand behind his back and walks stage right. Ruse eases Feast into a crouch behind a big sandbag, out of the Performer's view.

On the stage only a few feet away, the Performer throws open a nonexistent door. He bows and beckons someone in, moving out of their way and closing the door behind them. He twists his left hand as though locking the door with a key.

Then he guides his invisible visitor forward to stand beside the table. He sneaks behind them, bringing his right hand around and up. He prepares to stab the knife downward into their back.

*Look out!* Ruse shouts with a dampened voice. She immediately feels foolish, but she really thought one of those dough giants was standing in front of the Performer, oblivious to the danger it's in.

The Performer suddenly looks surprised and drops his hand behind his back again, hiding the knife. He whistles innocently, glancing back at his imaginary guest. He shrugs and shakes his head. Ruse giggles.

Feast shakes her shoulder. She reluctantly takes her eyes off the Performer. Feast gestures at something on the wall next to them. She doesn't see anything that he does until he gently takes her hand and places it on a metal bar. She looks closer: It's the rung of a ladder, painted black so it's almost invisible against the black walls, especially in the dark.

She cranes her neck, looking straight up. All she can make out is the spotlight and some elevated platforms high above them. They would be able to see more of the theater from there, the better to find additional exits, as well as stay out of the Performer's reach. It might also make it easier to spot Mim. She points up and Feast waves her on. He turns back to watch the stage.

So Ruse climbs. Halfway up, she pauses and looks down. She feels exposed up here, but the audience remains focused on the Performer. He is no longer preoccupied with his imaginary guest, and Ruse is annoyed to have missed part of the show. The Performer is now chopping something on the center table with the imaginary knife, periodically picking something up to hang on hooks in the ceiling.

When Ruse reaches the top of the ladder, she steps onto the metal catwalk around the theater's walls. She starts looking for a way out.

Suddenly a second spotlight shines onto the stage. Ruse leans over the edge of the suspended walkway to get a better look. The wooden crate is open now and the Performer is lifting something out of it.

Mim. Her eyes are closed and her arms are crossed over her chest.

The Performer gently stands her up on the stage. She's stiff and unmoving—until she starts tipping to the left. He hurries to catch her before she falls, and stands her upright again. She starts tipping to the right.

Despite herself, Ruse laughs silently. From the flapping mouths of the quelled audience, she isn't the only one. The audience is eating it up.

*Why isn't she running?* Ruse thinks.

The Performer repeats this charade a few more times, with the motionless Mim starting to fall forward and then backward. He throws his hands up in the air in frustration, then holds her in place with one hand on the top of her head. He taps his chin thoughtfully with a finger, then points the finger up in the air with a delighted expression, as if struck by a brilliant idea.

He reaches one hand into the box and retracts it, finger and thumb pressed together like he's holding something. He places his hand behind Mim's back and twists his wrist over and over, the way Ruse used to wind her pocket watch each morning.

When the Performer is finished, Mim starts walking forward, legs and arms stiff. She marches toward the edge of the stage. The Performer reacts, his mouth a wide, surprised O, and he rushes around to the front of the stage to catch her. He gently turns her around and she starts walking in the opposite direction. She bumps into the crate a few times, turning incrementally to her right until she is free to walk toward that edge.

Ruse giggles. Though she makes no noise except in her head, Mim pauses on the stage and her eyes flit up and find her. The Performer looks up too, his eyes narrowing to slits. Ruse covers her mouth and drops onto her stomach until he turns back to the stage.

Mim is walking again but more slowly than before. She continues to slow down until she stops and bends over with her arms down and freezes.

The Performer reaches into an invisible pocket but doesn't seem to find what he's looking for. He tries another pocket, patting his hands all over his body, increasingly frantic. He checks the table, scrutinizing every inch of it closely, feeling along the top of it. He leans down to the crate and sticks his head into it. When he stands up, his hat is gone.

The Performer stares out at the audience, peering out at them in confusion. They seem to be laughing at him. His face shows creeping realization and he slowly places his hand on his bare, curly head, probing with his fingers. He jumps when he discovers his hat is gone, and he starts the whole production all over again, looking around for it.

The audience becomes restless. Ruse can't hear them grumbling, but they seem less interested in the show when Mim isn't part of it. The Performer is losing control of the audience.

Anger flashes across his face and he stomps over to

the box. He yanks his hat out and slams it on his head. Ruse feels unsettled, like when her parents got so mad at her they stopped talking to her. Sometimes they even pretended she wasn't there, and more than once they left her alone in the house for the night. As they did on that last night.

Ruse reels from the unexpected memory, as sharp as a slap across the face. She now recalls how her parents looked—when they were angry. Ruse blinks away the blur in her vision and continues watching the Performer. She can tell that he isn't playing anymore. He's only going through the motions of his routine.

He picks up his hat and looks into it. A moment later, he rummages a hand inside and pulls out the invisible key. He replaces the hat and leans over to wind Mim up again. Mim straightens up and turns to face the audience. Feast tenses, but he can't get to Mim without being seen by everyone, and she's now standing right in front of the Performer.

The Performer bows, and Mim bows. He lifts his beret, and she tips an invisible hat of her own. Only her pained eyes betray her terror.

Ruse catches Feast looking up. *What do we do?* she mouths.

He shrugs.

The Performer continues to make Mim perform. With one leg straight out in front of her, she moves her hands up and down, fingers closing and opening like she's catching and throwing invisible objects. Matching the gestures of the Performer as he juggles five black apples over her head.

Maybe if Ruse can turn off those spotlights, Feast can usher Mim away in the dark while the Performer and the audience are distracted and blind. She works her way around the catwalk toward the first spotlight. When she reaches it, she is stunned to discover it's being operated by a kid.

The other child is a little taller than her, dressed in

tattered clothes: a white shirt, blue vest and pants, dusty black shoes. On their oversized head is a brimmed black hat with a red band and some kind of loop sticking out of the flat top. Their brown hands draw her attention the most as they guide the spotlight to follow Mim below. There is something odd about those hands and their jerky movements.

Ruse cautiously approaches. Closer up, she realizes that the hands are wooden with stiff, jointed fingers like a puppet's. She is startled when the figure snaps their head around to look at her.

It isn't a child at all. It isn't even alive. It *can't* be alive: Its face is sickly gray, messy white paint and rouge smeared over carved, sagging features. Instead of eyes it has empty black sockets, and uneven white teeth protrude from a wide mouth. Its thick, sneering lips part as a hinged jaw drops open.

*How is it moving?* she wonders. Then it turns the spotlight on her instead of the stage.

Ruse throws up an arm to shield her eyes, but for an agonizing moment, she can't see. She feels the vibration of something hard hitting the metal walkway in front of her and she blindly steps back, trying to keep her balance.

As her vision returns, she glances down in time to dodge a black apple that whooshes past her head. She avoids looking at the Performer directly, wary of being drawn into his act again. Instead, she watches Mim on the edge of the cold circle of light around him. The girl looks furious, like Ruse has never seen her before—mirroring the Performer's rage. She raises an empty, clawed hand, and pitches it forward. Another apple arcs through the air toward the catwalk, thrown by the Performer. This one hits the animated Puppet, knocking it backward. Below, Mim covers her eyes in embarrassment.

Before Ruse can change her mind, she darts past the Puppet struggling back to its feet, toward the spotlight.

She stands in front of the bright, hot bulb, squinting and waiting for Mim to chuck another invisible apple. She waits a beat and then ducks.

An apple zips over her head and into the spotlight, smashing the bulb with a fountain of yellow sparks. One down, one to go.

Ruse quickly closes the distance between her and the second spotlight, which is still focused on the Performer. She hopes Feast is ready to act under the cover of darkness.

This spotlight is operated by another marionette, with a sneer carved into his face. He looks ready to lunge at Ruse, but then his hands seem to move involuntarily, despite his cut strings. He swings the light up and over to the end of the catwalk. It illuminates a familiar banded door painted on a wall. Ruse's mouth parts in surprise as it opens and the Performer steps out onto the catwalk, his eyes on her. The metal shifts and sways beneath his weight.

Ruse quickly averts her gaze downward. In the dim light, she sees Feast trying to hold on to Mim, but the girl is again marching toward the edge of the stage and dragging him along with her, in lockstep with the Performer advancing toward Ruse on her right. The Puppet closes in on Ruse from her left.

There's only one direction Ruse can go: down. She grabs a black cable snaking across the catwalk with both hands. And she jumps.

As Ruse drops, one end of the cable breaks free of the spotlight and the bulb cuts out. Darkness settles over the auditorium, but Ruse is still falling, swinging, toward the stage.

She descends faster, arcing out over the audience, and then she's tumbling, rolling, sliding across the stage before coming to a rest, sprawled breathlessly on her back.

The audience starts booing and jeering.

She can hear them!

Beneath their displeasure, she hears a door creak open and then slam shut from high up in the rafters. The lights come up as a speaker crackles. A voice announces, "Thank you for attending our performance. Please exit to the rear of the theater."

Ruse sits up and takes everything in. The Performer is gone. The double doors are open and the audience is slowly tottering out into the lobby, making low snuffling sounds.

Upstage of Ruse, Feast and Mim huddle together, and Mim's hands cover her face. Ruse staggers back to her feet and moves unsteadily toward them.

"Okay?" Ruse asks. She smiles when Feast and Mim turn toward her. Her voice is back.

Mim doesn't respond until Ruse retrieves the rope from her pocket and lays it across Mim's lap. The other girl picks it up and cradles it close to her chest, like a baby doll. They wait that way together until the theater is empty. Ruse taps a finger on the stage and listens closely, hoping that the Performer will not return before they leave.

Finally, Ruse, Feast, and Mim clamber down the stage and exit into the theater lobby. The shabby red carpet is littered with greasy cardboard containers, crushed cups, and glistening crumbs. No one is around. Even the concession counter is abandoned, the grill behind it still sizzling with gray cubes that turn Ruse's stomach. Even so, she notices Feast gazing longingly at the food as they pass.

They hurry outside into a driving rain that pelts them with heavy, stinging drops. Dark clouds blot the horizon, and the soaked ground shimmers beneath flickering fairy lights strung up all around them. This section of the carnival is crowded with yellow-wheeled caravans, all shuttered against the weather.

The air smells like a wet campfire. Is the hedge maze nearby? It should be just on the other side of this theater, but it's impossible to tell where they are, or where they should go, without reaching higher ground.

"Should we wait?" Feast whispers.

Ruse glances at Mim. Her face is pale, almost ghostly, and there are dark shadows around her now listless eyes. It seems best to get her away from this place, and hope the Performer does not follow.

Ruse shades her eyes with her hand and looks around. The Giant Wheel is closer now, still lit up but unmoving. But there's another way to get above the carnival to scout it out. She points to a roller-coaster track looming nearby, silhouetted against the stormy sky.

Feast sighs. But he takes Mim's limp hand, and, with Ruse leading the way this time, they head for the tracks.

# CHAPTER 6

**Ruse, Feast, and Mim trudge up the wooden** tracks of the roller coaster, climbing higher and higher above the carnival.

Ruse keeps checking over her shoulder as they ascend. She has an itchy sensation at the back of her skull, like she's once more being watched. Perhaps she isn't the only one: Mim's attention has been squarely fixed on the squat theater they left near the empty roller-coaster cars, so she keeps stepping on her own feet as Feast pulls her alongside him.

Ruse stumbles, a reminder to direct her attention forward and pick her way carefully. The only illumination comes from floodlights aimed up at the tracks, lanterns and fairy lights strung up around the fairgrounds below, and lights from scattered caravans and stalls. The carnival might be pretty if the tents and ramshackle buildings didn't list and twist into odd shapes, casting ominous shadows.

And there are other things that don't seem to belong in a fair, like tall wooden poles with ropes stretched between them, and even some sort of lookout tower with a crow's nest on top. The way the storm clouds race by on the horizon makes her feel like time is moving much too fast, or that the carnival *itself* is somehow moving. She feels both lightheaded and heavy all at once, slightly off-balance. Which makes it even harder to keep her footing on the tracks, especially while looking for somewhere safe to go.

On her right is a huge circus tent. The canvas has a

warm glow from the lights within. Vertical red-and-white stripes converge in a single spire, from which a black pennant flutters. *There must be a show going on*, Ruse thinks. It would be a shelter from the rain, but she expects there are more of those dough people gathered inside, watching another performance. She'll take her chances outside. Nothing else is moving about in this dreary weather. But the rain is clearing up and they could have company soon.

The motionless Giant Wheel looms to their left, lights twinkling around its circumference. The top of it is higher than the coaster tracks. Closer by, the charred remains of the paper hedge maze are smoldering in the rain. From up here, the scorched ground forms the shape of an enormous eye.

It might just be the lingering acrid smoke, but even the air here is *wrong*: It smells stale and leaves a bitter taste in her mouth. It feels thinner than it should, so she works harder to breathe. It's like slowly drowning on land.

Ruse turns to ask Feast if he smells something bad, but she holds her tongue when she sees the cloth mask over his face. He'd had an unpleasant odor when she met him, but she must have gotten used to it, or everything else smells far worse.

Even with half his face hidden, it's obvious that Feast is unwell. His usually sharp eyes seem distant and unfocused, and he walks with his free hand pressed into his stomach. He needs to eat soon. Ruse can't remember when she last ate, but she doesn't feel hungry, at least not for anything in this carnival. Maybe food will be more appealing outside it.

Ruse continues to lead the others up the roller-coaster tracks. As she crests the top of the hill, she holds her breath to take in the expansive view. She should be able to see what lies outside the carnival, but beyond it is nothing but dark sky and clouds.

She lets her breath out in a sigh. *That's not possible*, she thinks.

She again notices those unusual poles spaced around the fairgrounds. Some of them have crossbeams with dangling ropes and tattered fabric flapping in the wind. They remind her of a sailing ship. She remembers the hollow sound of her feet on the ground as if they were not on dirt but on wood.

*Like a ship's deck.*

Ruse spins around slowly, taking it all in. "We're in the air," she says. "This is a flying carnival."

Questions buzz through her head. How can a ship fly? Why does it have a carnival? How did they get here?

How would they get *down*?

Her companions are as stunned as she is. Even Mim's eyes have gone round with wonder. She guesses that wherever they're from, they've never seen a ship in the sky either. No one has ever seen anything like this over The Counties. Ruse scans the unnervingly empty horizon for some clue to where they are. Then something rises into view in the distance.

It's long and lemon shaped, but a dingy brown with a gondola dangling below it. Propellers spin all over it as it slowly circles the fairgrounds.

*What is that?* she thinks. It looks like a giant balloon. *Did that bring us here?*

Ruse stares at the balloon as it dips out of sight again on the opposite side of the carnival. She wonders if there are other levels below and how to get to them.

"That's our way out," she says softly.

Feast raises an eyebrow.

"It must dock somewhere to drop off and pick up people." They need to find it. Although the carnival itself must land from time to time, she's unwilling to wait any longer to leave it. Feast glances at Mim, who has once again focused on the theater where she had been part of the Performer's act. He looks back at Ruse and nods.

The other side of the track is too steep a drop for them to climb down without slipping and falling, so she turns around. It will take a long time to go all the way back down the way they came. She almost trips over Mim, who is crouching over the rail with her ear pressed against it.

Ruse starts to say something, but Mim holds up a hand to silence her. Ruse bites her lip. Then Mim puts her hand on the rail next to her ear.

Ruse crouches and presses her hand against the wet metal. She feels a barely perceptible vibration. The metal softly hums.

She looks up. The rain is gone and the rides are back in service. Carnival music picks up and the Giant Wheel begins to turn.

Feast is looking down the slope with a worried look on his face. Ruse joins him and sees that the roller coaster has just left the loading station and is rumbling slowly along the tracks, pulled by a chain or cable up the incline. It has five dark red cars, and all but the last one has a dough giant crammed into it, their flesh spilling over the sides of a seat too small for them.

The coaster will run them over any moment.

Ruse hops down onto a track and waves for the others to join her. Feast helps Mim climb off the rail and the rotting wood splinters ominously beneath their combined weight. It groans and shifts from the vibration of the approaching cars.

And then it's upon them.

Ruse digs her back into the wooden slat and the first car of the coaster rolls harmlessly over her. The bottom of it is only an inch from her nose. She dares not move, doesn't even breathe while the train passes. Her heart thuds in rhythm with the coaster's wheels.

In a blink, the first car passes, then the second. Car number three.

As the fourth car rolls by, the coaster slows down. And just as the fifth car nudges past Ruse, it stops, teetering on the summit before continuing down the hill. Ruse has a sudden idea and is already up and moving as she whispers to Feast and Mim, "Let's get on."

"What?" Feast says. But they don't have much time to act, and Ruse is already beginning to climb aboard. She hopes that Feast will make the split decision to follow her lead.

A breath later, she's relieved when he crawls out from under the coaster, coaxing Mim along with him, and the three of them climb over the back of the fifth car and drop into the wicker seat inside. They're too short to see over the sides, but a dough giant is stuffed into the car ahead of them, his massive back and hunched shoulders blotting out his head.

Ruse and the others grip the edge of their seat as the coaster dips over the summit. She experiences a brief sensation of weightlessness as the train plummets downward, feeling it pick up speed as it reaches the bottom before it then continues up another hill, curving to the left so that the Giant Wheel whirls by along with streaking carnival lights.

Incredible pressure pushes Ruse backward. The

rattling of the rickety old coaster suggests it is barely holding together. Even her teeth and bones vibrate from the motion.

Then she is lifted off the seat and her fingers ache with the effort of keeping herself from being ripped away like a kite in high winds.

Ruse grits her teeth, swallowing the scream in her throat. While the train is descending, she can see all four cars ahead—and below—them. The bulky riders raise their arms and make low, guttural sounds as the coaster falls. The track stretches a long way before them at a steep angle before it levels out at the bottom.

They hit the flat straightaway and Ruse comes crashing down again, suddenly feeling four times as heavy. She grunts as her knees bump on the hard bench. The train continues around the curving track, heading for another shorter hill with a gentler incline.

Soon the coaster rockets up along that short stretch

of track to another peak, which means another descent is imminent.

The roller coaster descends in a tight spiral. The car is shaking and rumbling so violently she wonders if it's even going to make it to the end of the line.

The coaster reaches the ground and lights from carnival attractions pass by in a blur of colors above for the final stretch. Suddenly they're plunged into total darkness as they enter a tunnel.

Ruse's stomach drops as the coaster abruptly shifts downward. Over the screeching wheels, she hears a metallic slicing sound followed by a *bump, bump, bump, bump*. Something whistles past just over her head. Then the coaster begins to brake, the rails sending showers of sparks and flashes of light that illuminate the tunnel like a series of black-and-white photos.

The rider in front of her seems shorter, perhaps ducking to clear the very low ceiling of the tunnel. But then she is holding tight to her seat again as the coaster abruptly twists and flips upside down. It trembles and she hears four wet *thunks* below her before it rights itself and emerges from the tunnel, coming to a lurching stop at an unloading station platform.

The dough giant who had been sitting in front of them is gone. Ruse shakily stands on the seat to look over the front of the car and is astonished to discover that the first four coaster cars are now empty.

Mim whimpers beside her. Feast is purposefully looking away from the coaster, rubbing his arms and wincing. Ruse flexes her hands and stretches her aching muscles.

The coaster clicks and shudders. Then it jerks forward, slowly advancing past the station stop. Ruse hurriedly leaps clear of the car, tumbling out onto the platform. The wind gets knocked out of her and she is suddenly back in the water, sinking deeper into its cold, murky depths. Above her two bodies float on the surface, getting smaller and smaller as she goes deeper and slips away . . .

She startles awake, coughing, to find Feast leaning

over her with concerned eyes. “Breathe,” he murmurs.

She couldn’t have been out for long because the riderless coaster cars are still rumbling up the track to pick up a fresh load of carnival-goers. Ruse lets Feast help her up and she looks for Mim. The girl is staring at an adjoining building with a flashing sign over closed red doors. Ruse tries to read it but can’t understand the words. One letter, illegible on its own, has fallen to the deck. A cacophony of bells and whistles spills from a broken window, and more of that familiar carnival tune, played by bass instruments and an accordion. Ruse has a strong sense that there are games inside.

Ruse is surprised when Mim runs toward the entrance, leaving her and Feast behind.

“Hey!” Ruse calls. But Mim doesn’t stop, and Feast takes a few tentative steps after her. He looks back at Ruse.

She sighs, then picks herself up and dusts off her clothes. They hurry to catch up to Mim.

# CHAPTER 7

**The doors are chained and padlocked, and** rusted chain-link fences on either side of the building prevent them from going around. Ruse tries to picture the layout of the carnival from her time on the roller-coaster tracks. She feels certain the balloon ship landed just on the other side of the game room. That's where they need to go.

Ruse turns her mind to figuring out how to enter the building, but Mim and Feast are already dragging the fallen letter to the broken window. Ruse helps them position it to form steps they can climb to the sill. Mim charges up them, with Feast on her heels.

Ruse clambers after them, wondering what has so captured Mim's interest. Though they haven't spent much time together, the other girl hasn't been acting like herself.

Careful to avoid the jagged glass protruding from the window's wooden frame, Ruse steps through the hole onto a barrel top on the other side. She wrinkles her nose at the sour stench of sweat and rotting vegetation. The loud, discordant music would have had Mim curled up with fingers plugged into her ears earlier, but she seems oblivious to the noise. She hops down to the deck and walks toward the carnival stands, brightly lit in the otherwise dim arcade. Feast trails after her uncertainly.

Mim approaches the first booth. It's striped red and white like the carnival tents, and behind a counter, glass bottles are arranged with blue rings around their necks.

Ruse has a vague memory of her father explaining how the ring toss works, as an excuse for not letting her play any of the games at the Hatefields Fair. Some of the bottles already had rings on them to make players think it's easy to succeed. But the bottles are set up to hide that they're actually larger than the rings that are given to throw, making it impossible to win.

As Mim passes the ring toss counter, a figure vaults over it and lands in front of her with a wooden clatter. Mim stumbles backward but Feast catches her, and they huddle together looking up at the animated doll in shock.

He's dressed similarly to the Puppet Ruse saw in the theater, with severed strings dangling from his straw hat, hands, and feet and a downturned smile. Her companions had been down on the stage, so they haven't seen anything like it before. And it seems that this Puppet hasn't seen anything like *them* either. He studies the cowering children, tilting his leering face curiously and making disturbing croaking sounds. Is he attempting to speak?

He stalks toward Feast and Mim with jerky motions, feet *clomping* hollowly on the deck.

The kids back away and then dart behind the ring toss booth while Ruse heads for the opposite booth. Objects fall and glass shatters behind her. Running footsteps echo, barely audible over the music in the arcade.

Ruse slips through a flap at the back of the booth and finds herself behind the counter, among a pile of stuffed teddy bears. One of the prizes has an open seam in the back; instead of cotton, it is stuffed with silver needles. Above Ruse is a table with bottles stacked on it. She accidentally nudges a wooden ball. She picks it up and finds it's lighter than it looks, probably so it can't knock over the bottles, which she feels confident are also stuck together.

*Clomp.* A second Puppet drops down from the counter and reaches out for her. She smashes his scowling face in with the ball, cracking both it and his head. He stumbles backward into the table and collapses. The bottles above him wobble but do not fall.

Ruse wriggles under the canvas wall into the next booth over. This one has a hoop with a large leather ball beneath it. She bumps it as she sneaks past, and footsteps thump toward her. She ducks under the counter and hides. The shadow of a Puppet appears on the back wall and lingers. She holds her breath until it moves on.

She lifts the bottom of the booth's canvas wall and faces a row of mechanical marble game tables on the other side. A Puppet crouches on the glass top of one, facing away from her. She retreats back into the tent and lifts the ball onto the counter. She gives it a gentle push and it rolls down its length before dropping over the edge and bouncing away.

Several Puppets clatter after it and she quickly slides out of the tent and crouch-runs into the shadows beneath the first marble game. She crawls under the row of tables, out of sight of the Puppets standing around the leather ball in the middle of the arcade, looking around for her.

There are too many to handle on her own. Perhaps too many even for her, Mim, and Feast combined. Yet she feels stronger in their company. Working together is their only hope of defending themselves.

Ruse reaches the last table and peeks around the edge, watching and waiting. She catches quick movement on the other side of the room. Feast and Mim! They disappear behind another machine that reminds her of a miniature bowling alley, only it seems like Ruse would have to roll balls up the lane into various circles.

Feast peers around the machine and spots Ruse. His eyes crinkle in relief, mirroring Ruse's feelings about them finding each other. He nods his head down the arcade and Ruse risks standing up long enough to look. There are two double doors on the far end of the arcade, just past a ball pit. Ruse nods. She'll meet them there.

But first she has to get past a Puppet standing in front of what looks like a small garden. It's holding a large wooden mallet. Just beyond the garden, there's a support pillar she can hide behind. If she can sneak across to it.

Ruse tiptoes into the garden when the Puppet is looking the other way. As soon as she steps onto the spongy soil, machinery below clicks and rumbles and several fleshy gray grubs with human mouths and teeth pop out of holes around her. She hops behind one of them as the Puppet whirls around.

*WHAM!*

The mallet smashes down the motorized grub on her left, forcing it back into the ground. Hidden machinery begins ticking and—*WHAM!*—the mallet smacks another grub on the board.

*WHAM! WHAM!*

The ticking increases and Ruse hears gears and springs engage at her feet. As soon as the grubs retract into the ground, she'll be exposed.

*WHAM!*

Another grub goes down on her right. Ruse wraps her arms around the grub in front of her and slides down the space between it and the hole.

*Tchk, tchk, tchk.* The remaining grubs all drop back to their positions below the surface.

Ruse crawls beneath turning gears and squeezes through tight crevices in the machinery, thinking this must be what it's like inside a clock. Mechanisms slide into place and she hears a twang of springs and pistons as another assortment of grubs pop out into the open.

*WHAM! WHAM!*

She dashes under a grub and nearly gets clipped by it as the Puppet hammers it back down. She isn't safe above and she isn't safe below.

The machinery resets and fires once more while she works her way across. By listening to the springs being loaded before they engage, she thinks she can predict which of the grubs are going to emerge in each round.

When she reaches the other side of the game, the machinery ticks once more as the grubs are primed. She hears a telltale soft click in the grub behind, so she whips around and grabs hold of it—and when it launches, she rides it up out of the hole.

*WHAM!* Another grub goes down and Ruse hops down to make a run for the square black pillar ahead, almost invisible in the darkness.

*WHAM!* The mallet hits the deck on her heels, but Ruse doesn't stop. The Puppet clatters after her. She reaches the pillar and ducks down in the shadows on its other side. The Puppet runs past without seeing her crouching in the shadows. She notices that its wooden feet no longer make the *clip-clop* of a galloping horse.

In fact, the entire arcade is quiet now. She had gotten so used to the constant noise that she stopped noticing it—until it wasn't there anymore.

*Oh no*, she says silently. She steps forward and slowly turns to look around the entire room. She gasps when she sees a striped door painted on the pillar she was just hiding behind.

*He's here. But where?*

Mim.

Ruse races to the doors at the back of the arcade, grateful for the silence that masks her footsteps from the Puppets. But they aren't paying attention to her anyway. Four of the wooden marionettes are watching Mim intently, but not attacking. She's punching, feinting, and dodging as if fighting an invisible opponent.

In her peripheral vision, in the shadows, Ruse sees the Performer's ghostly face and white hands curled into fists mirroring Mim's movements—boxing the air. It's his act the Puppets are watching.

Ruse creeps closer. Beyond the distracted Puppets, she spots Feast standing at the base of a game that tests your strength. He's swinging a wooden mallet to fend off a Puppet following the same motions as Mim and the Performer. Feast scores a hit on the Puppet's head, and it collapses. It lies still for a moment and then climbs back onto its feet. Feast readies the mallet again, but another Puppet from the group steps up to join the first. Then another. And another. And another. Their actions are no longer synchronized, but they remain focused on fighting Feast.

The Performer is walking away, tilted forward at a forty-five-degree angle with a hand up to shield his eyes, the other hand clapping his beret onto his head. In that fashion, he and Mim force their way through a nonexistent gale toward the doors at the back of the arcade.

If Ruse goes after Mim, could she pull her away from the Performer's control the way Feast had?

Whatever the Performer's plans are for Mim, for the moment he seems to want to include her in his act. As unthinkable as it is to leave her under his power, Feast is in more immediate jeopardy, so she should help him first. Besides, Ruse thinks she may need him to recover Mim.

A Puppet seizes Feast from behind and holds the boy's arms to his side, forcing him to drop his mallet. Feast breaks free and turns to kick the Puppet, knocking it down. He lunges for the mallet but another Puppet tackles him to the deck, pinning him to the ground.

The wide rear doors of the arcade open before the Performer and Mim. Ruse glimpses only the empty horizon beyond the threshold.

Ruse decides. "We'll find you!" she calls out silently. Is it just her imagination or does the girl look back at her as she follows her captor out of the arcade?

Sound rushes back, and she hears Feast yell, "Help!"

Three Puppets have tied him up with string and are dragging him along the ground. The boy twists and squirms, but he settles down when he notices Ruse sneaking after them. She puts a finger to her lips and follows as they carry him to a large pit brimming with black, gray, and white balls in a corner to the left of the exit. A climbing cargo net is draped against the adjoining walls.

In the back of her mind, Ruse's instincts shout that this seemingly playful attraction is unnatural and dangerous. She is somehow sure that if Feast slips below the inviting surface of spheres, he will disappear in the pit's hidden depths, never to be seen again.

They toss Feast in.

"No!" Ruse rushes to the edge of the pit and stretches a hand down to grab him. He's just out of reach, and with his arms bound he can't take her hand or keep himself on the surface. The more he thrashes around, the faster the balls shift and cascade over him.

Feast's terrified eyes are the last Ruse sees of him before the bottomless pit swallows him.

# CHAPTER 8

**At the edge of the ball pit, with the Puppets** closing in on her, Ruse tries to leap after Feast—but she can't. As much as she wants to, her body won't move. It doesn't feel like an outside force is controlling her, like the Performer's power over Mim. It's something deep inside her.

Dread.

But she's not afraid about what *might* happen. It's more like part of her somehow knows what comes next, even if her brain doesn't. This buried knowledge paralyzes her—she can't even breathe. Her heart pounds loud, fast, and steady: ticking away precious time. Every second counts if she's to rescue Feast.

She gasps and coughs, abruptly able to move again. When she recovers, she finds she's clenching her pocket watch. It reminds her of where all this began. She tucks away the watch again like a secret and then takes a deep breath.

She jumps.

Hitting the surface is nothing like jumping into a pool. She thought it might hurt, but the wooden balls are hollow and light, so she slips between them easily.

Too easily.

The momentum from her dive carries her down the pit quickly. She learns she can move through the balls with wide arm movements and cupped hands, to sweep the balls behind her and propel herself. It's slow and takes much more effort than swimming in water. It's exhausting. Not only physically, but emotionally.

Another familiar feeling creeps into her mind: despair.

She pushes harder.

It's suffocating down here. There's air, but she can't get enough of it. *I'm drowning again*, she thinks.

She stops moving, caught up in another returning memory.

*Sinking, sinking, sinking in Nanny's pool. She knows how to swim, so why doesn't she? She jumped and now she's here and soon she'll be nowhere.*

*She reaches the bottom and waits, bubbles of air slipping from her lips. Then, with a start, she kicks off from the bottom. She swims back to the top, but she never reaches the surface. She can't. No matter how much she kicks and moves her arms, something holds her back. Pushes her down. Something dark in the pool with her that can't, won't let go. Will never let go.*

Ruse is sinking, sinking, sinking in the ball pit. She kicks her legs and moves her arms in wide circular motions to stop her descent. The wooden balls clacking against one another make it difficult to think. She jumped into the pit without having a plan to help Feast. How can she even find him? She looks around, but the light filtering through from above is weak and she can't see much.

She pauses and gradually starts to slip downward again, the hollow balls clicking against one another softly as they shift around her. But she stays perfectly still until she hears something. On her right, slightly below her, there's a louder rattle of balls as something moves in the pit.

"Feast?" she calls. Her voice is muffled, most of the sound bouncing back to her.

Why doesn't he answer?

She heads where she thinks he is, pausing periodically to listen and adjust her direction. She hears . . .

Rain?

That can't be right, but the sound reminds her of raindrops against a windowpane. She flicks a fingernail against a wooden ball near her hand. The tapping is similar. The balls in the pit are knocking against something hard nearby, maybe the side of the pit?

She senses a shadow moving below her accompanying the rain-like sound. She can tell it's humongous, displacing a large number of balls in its wake. The shifting spheres push Ruse up and to the side, turning her head upside down and disorienting her.

*What is that?*

She holds herself very still until it passes.

She's now paranoid about moving, but she doesn't have a choice. She'll just have to be faster.

Ruse keeps heading toward what she hopes is Feast. In the pit's depths, it gets darker and darker, the balls pressing against her more heavily. She struggles even more with each stifling breath. Surely, she should have reached the bottom of the ship by now. She has the impossible impression that there's no end to this pit, that it continues down forever.

She is about to go back up in defeat when she finally

spots Feast in front of her. He isn't moving. She kicks hard and wraps her arm around his chest. She tows him alongside her as she swims frantically—not toward the surface, which is a slow, losing battle, but toward the side of the pit. It may not have a bottom, but the pit has walls.

Feeling like she has been swimming for days, like she has *always* been swimming, her outstretched hand finally bumps against a wall. She feels around until her fingers finally hook into something. *The climbing net*, she thinks.

She pulls herself and Feast over to the wall and finds a foothold. She climbs the net. One laborious rung at a time.

Her lungs burn and her arms feel numb and heavy. She expects a strong, cold hand to hold her down, shove her back into the depths. But she keeps moving.

Finally, she breaks the surface of the ball pit. She pulls Feast up and rests him on the top layer to catch her breath and recover her strength. The spheres support him for a moment, but then he rapidly slides back down into them, out of her grasp.

*No!* she thinks.

Ruse clings to the net, knuckles white, and strains to reach him. Before he vanishes completely, she lets go and lunges for him.

She grabs hold of his arm and holds him up, then drags him back toward the wall and grabs onto the net with her free hand. She shakes Feast gently, but his eyes remain closed. She's considering removing his mask to check on him when he rasps. His chest slowly rises and falls and then, weakly, he says, "Ruse?"

"I'm here." Balls in the pit rattle and clack against one another. Ruse follows the sound with her eyes to the other end of the pool, where wooden balls are rippling. Something very big is just beneath the surface. The spheres settle and she scans around looking for another surge.

She hooks her leg into the net for stability and tries to free Feast from his bonds. The string is too tightly knotted, so she tears it apart with her teeth as another swell appears and slowly moves toward them.

The last of the string drops away and Ruse guides Feast onto the net beside her. Then something brushes against her leg. She startles and twists away from it. She tries to climb the wall, but the thing has hold of one of her legs. She kicks but can't break free of it.

She hangs on the net with one hand, Feast grabbing the other.

"Go!" she shouts to him. He shakes his head but pulls her hand free from his. "Save Mim."

She holds on tight to the rung of the net as the thing tries to drag her back down into the ball pit. Her fingers ache and her joints pop from the stress of being stretched like taffy. She can't hold on much longer.

Above her, she tracks Feast as he sidles along the wall toward the exit of the arcade. The Puppets ignore him now, focused on watching Ruse. She's relieved when the thing suddenly lets go of her—until it begins tugging the net away from the wall instead. The net stretches far out over the pit, with her dangling from it by both hands. The balls below her churn loudly.

With a *snap*, the cargo net is torn from the wall and drops over the pit, along with Ruse. The netting settles across the bobbing surface of balls. Ruse jumps up and runs along the ropes as quickly as she can, toward the edge of the pit. Before she gets there, her ankle gets tangled in rope and she trips. Now she's being carried back to the center of the pit, where the net is being pulled down.

She can't feel her fingers anymore, but she must still be holding on to the net. She tries to pull herself free, but her arms are leaden. She can't do it. She can't go on.

She knew this would happen. *And I would do it again anyway*, she thinks.

But then she feels small hands around her ankle. She

twists around and sees Feast there, trying to free her from the net.

He came back for her.

She watches anxiously as they draw closer to where the net is being sucked downward, but he quickly and calmly untangles her. He gestures for her to move, and they both jump into the pit, swimming frantically away from the thing below them.

With the net gone, Ruse hears the clatter of balls behind them. The surface undulates around them and it's all they can do to stay ahead of the thing beneath it in pursuit. But as soon as they reach the edge of the pit and clamber out onto the deck, the mound of balls subsides.

Breathing heavily, Ruse gasps out, "Thank you."

"You saved me first," Feast says.

She doesn't tell him that she nearly didn't. Knowing him, he would have done it anyway, without thinking of himself first. She wonders if that's how he had ended up in this place.

Feast looks behind her with alarm. She hears stomping feet and turns to see the Puppets advancing on them.

Feast reaches down and grabs an armful of balls. He chucks them at the Puppets moving around the pit. *Clop! Clop! Clop!* He has surprisingly good aim. He manages to hit one of the Puppets square in the face with a hollow *thunk*. It flails its arms and topples into the pit. If this had been a carnival game, he would have won a prize.

A shifting mound of balls veers toward the Puppet, which is standing unsteadily on the surface of the pit. The spheres collapse under the Puppet, pulling him down and closing over him. A moment later, a head, torso, and limbs are ejected in a geyser of black, white, and gray. Balls spill over the sides of the pit, bouncing and scattering across the floor.

Ruse feels a twinge of sympathy for the Puppet. She had nearly suffered a similar fate, escaping only because of Feast. Of course, she had put herself into danger for him in the first place—which was even more remarkable.

She had jumped into Nanny's pool fearlessly because she had nothing to lose. It had been harder to jump into the ball pit.

But they aren't out of danger yet. The Puppets are on the move again. Ruse and Feast need to get out of here.

Feast taps Ruse's shoulder. "Mim?" he says.

Ruse now feels that when the time is right, she wants to tell Feast about the pool and what little she remembers of her life before. She wonders, too, how he came here and if he'll be willing to share his past.

Ruse, realizing she hasn't answered Feast yet, points toward the back doors of the arcade where the Performer and Mim departed. Feast nods with determination. She joins hands with him and they run, racing the Puppets for the exit. Racing to save Mim.

# CHAPTER 9

**Ruse and Feast outpace the Puppets and** exit the arcade onto a loading dock. Wood crates are stacked high; hanging lanterns and low spotlights around them cast long shadows. Several inactive conveyor belts lead from a hatch in the deck, crisscrossing the space. One very long belt extends off the edge of the deck into a clear, starless sky.

Ruse scans the blank horizon. "Where's that balloon ship?" she asks disappointedly. They must have missed it.

Feast doesn't respond—because he doesn't hear her. Ruse doesn't hear anything either. Not the arcade games through the open doors, or the Giant Wheel spinning just beyond the dock. Not the blackbirds circling overhead. The Performer is near.

Ruse and Feast enter a canyon of crates, where the air is thick with a pungent odor that makes her gag. Eyes watering, she covers her nose and mouth with a hand, envying Feast and his mask. They search for Mim, hurrying along narrow, twisting paths between the boxes: the streets and alleys of a makeshift, miniature city. The towering wooden piles sway ominously from side to side, threatening to tip at any moment.

They step out to the other side of the stacked boxes. Ruse locates Mim first. The girl stands alone on a ramshackle stage assembled from more crates . . . but she's changed. Her face is painted white except for black smudges over her eyes.

*What has he done to her?* Ruse thinks. She peers around

the dock looking for the Performer or one of his doors until Feast points above them. There! The Performer stands on a crate dangling from a rope and pulley over the long conveyor belt. He watches Mim for a while, then bows with a flourish, steps backward, and drops from view. Ruse startles. He didn't fall from the crate, so where did he go?

Feast heads for Mim and clambers up the crates to the stage. Mim holds her hands out in front of her, sliding them up and down and over as though she's feeling an unseen wall. She turns to her left and walks a few steps, only to come up short and bounce back a little. She rubs her nose. When she swats at the air in front of her, her hand seems to smack against something solid.

Feast reaches for Mim, but he, too, comes up against an invisible barrier. He leans into it and walks, pounds at it, and kicks, but he cannot push past it and reach her. Has he become a part of *her* act?

A flapping crow drops down to the deck in front of

Ruse, snapping her out of a deepening trance. She looks away from the stage and finds dozens of the large black-feathered birds have lit upon crates and conveyor belts around the loading dock. All of them are riveted by Mim's performance. Ruse risks a glance at Feast.

He's given up trying to get to Mim, just watching her trace the dimensions of the pretend prison she appears to be trapped in. The Performer can't be far. Ruse turns away from the spectacle and eyes the high-up crate where he'd disappeared. She traces the rope around it to a hook connected to a pulley, mounted on a simple metal hoist and arm mechanism. It seems impossible to get up there, but the Performer had managed it. She surveys the deck again. One of the crows is perched on a metal control panel she hadn't noticed before with multiple levers sticking out of it.

She hurries over and examines the levers and dials. She wraps both hands around one of the levers and yanks it down. The crow flaps indignantly and lifts away to a new perch as the conveyor belts begin moving. She switches them off again and tries spinning a dial. The crate tied above slowly swings to the right. She keeps it moving until it's lined up with the long conveyor belt. She yanks down on the lever near the pulley controls and the crate plummets straight down.

Ruse winces as it smashes into the conveyor belt and breaks open—accompanied by an audible *crack*, the first she's heard at the loading dock. Which must mean the Performer has gone away.

The sound and impact send the crows back into flight and tears Feast's attention away from Mim. Ruse waves at him, already running toward the broken crate.

"Don't look at her!" she shouts. Whether Feast hears her or figures it out for himself, he closes his eyes against Mim's act. He cups his hands around his mouth—his mask—and leans forward, shouting something to try to get through to her.

Ruse keeps moving down the conveyor belt. She

glances over the sides and is suddenly dizzy from the uninterrupted view of sky and clouds below.

Above her, the crows are circling the crate, and when she gets closer, she knows why. Bundles wrapped in paper and string have spilled out of the smashed wooden box. One of the birds lands on the conveyor belt and pecks at a package, tearing the paper and pulling sinewy, glistening strands from it. Ruse grimaces and explores the wreckage of the crate. She doesn't know what she's looking for until she finds it: One of the broken sides of the box has a painting of the Performer's door.

If he dropped through this before, it's closed now. But there's a crack running down the image, wide enough for Ruse to squeeze through. She puts her eye to it and sees a light within.

Ruse crawls inside.

On the other side is a room with four mirrored walls and a mirrored ceiling. The only things in it are a gramophone, a wooden chair—and the Performer, duplicated infinitely in the reflective surfaces. She isn't even sure where he is in the room, but she forces herself to look at him only in the mirrors.

She's seen this room before, from below. There's the vent, right below the gramophone. And as before, the Performer is acting out a routine: exactly the same one as Mim on the loading dock stage. He's holding his hands to the walls, caressing his own reflection in the glass. The only thing marring them is the crack in the mirror Ruse has just crawled through, which seems to be spreading slowly up the wall.

The Performer seems to sense her presence, all of his reflections turning to find her. He makes a grab for her. She scampers away, not certain which of his images is the real one. Infinite other Ruses scatter with her. The Performer bumps into a mirror, and his reflections all pause to rub their nose. But he turns and continues pursuing her as she runs around the edges of the room.

As she passes under the gramophone, she hears a burst of static and slides to a stop beneath it. The static is speaking. Shouting. It's saying, "Mim! Wake up!" It's Feast's voice. How can she hear him in here?

The unexpected sound seems to both paralyze and infuriate the Performer. He stops to cover his ears against Feast's voice. He's only able to advance in between Feast's calls.

*Don't stop, Feast*, Ruse thinks. She climbs the ornate gramophone table, nervously eyeing the reflections of the Performer as he gradually approaches it, step-by-step.

Ruse reaches the top of the gramophone, where a scratchy record turns. Feast's voice intermittently whispers from the speaker horn.

*"Mim!"*

Ruse grabs one of the many dials on the machine. If the sound pains the Performer, then . . .

She twists the dial, cranking up the volume.

The sound fuzzes and when Feast's voice calls

next—*"Mim!"*—the Performer clutches his head and staggers backward. Ruse reaches for another dial, but the Performer turns his attention to the gramophone. And her. He rushes toward the table and grabs for her. She ducks away behind the brass horn. She watches his distorted reflection turn the volume down. She tenses, and before he can compose himself, she darts back out again toward a metal slider nearby. She grabs hold of it and leans forward, pushing it all the way to the top. A shrill ring comes out of the gramophone, a blaring sound that peaks each time Feast's high-pitched voice shouts out:

*"MIM! WAKE UP!"*

The Performer, his face twisted in agony and anger, slams his hand down toward her. She rolls away from it and turns another dial all the way around.

"*MIM!*"

The Performer staggers backward, hands clamped over his ears. He struggles to recover against the onslaught, giving Ruse time to spin more dials, toggle switches, and push buttons.

"*MIM! PLEASE!*"

Ruse grimaces at the deafening noise, covering her own ears as the room begins trembling around them.

*Crack!* The mirrored walls splinter and crumble.

The Performer is on his knees in the center of the room, hunched over with his hands clamping his beret down over his ears. Ruse hops down and heads for the crack she came through, dodging shards of glass raining from the ceiling and shattering around her. Her face and hands sting as fragments of exploding glass pelt her. She raises an arm to protect her eyes, as much from the Performer as from cuts.

She has a moment of panic as she tries to locate the crack that will bring her back to Feast and Mim. As pieces of the mirrors fall away, she glimpses different rooms and spaces. She recognizes a fragment of the Performer's theater behind one jagged opening, the arcade behind another. But as an entire section of wall collapses, she sees only a chilling void. Other cracks reveal a seeking eye.

She finds the ever-widening crack that leads to the loading dock, and she dives through.

She tumbles out onto the conveyor belt and rolls to a stop. She climbs to her feet and carefully brushes glinting silver shards of glass from her hair and clothes.

She slowly makes her way over to her friends. Mim is off the stage, hunched over on the deck like the Performer while an agitated Feast tries to lift her to her feet. Then Mim begins crawling toward the conveyor belt. Toward Ruse.

Ruse feels that itch at the back of her head that tells her to look around. The Performer is crawling out of the painted door on the broken wooden lid on the conveyor belt. Deep slashes in his white face paint reveal that void Ruse glimpsed behind the broken mirrors. She feels like she's losing herself in them until the conveyor belt below her stutters to a start. It's moving, pulling her and the Performer backward toward the end of the dock.

Ruse turns and runs, making slow progress against the sliding platform. Up ahead, Mim is marching toward her, no doubt mirroring the Performer behind her, though she dare not look again. Beyond the girl, Feast is at the control panel, his hands on the lever that activated the belt. When he sees Ruse being pursued by the Performer, he races over to Mim, grabbing her shoulder to slow her down—without much effect. Ruse, Mim, and Feast meet on the conveyor belt. She hears the Performer continuing his pursuit, each of his footsteps like crunching glass. Sound warps around them, the carnival music and creaking Giant Wheel muffled. Feast's voice cuts in and out.

Ruse says quietly, "Mim?"

Mim blinks but has no other reaction as she continues to walk along the conveyor belt, forcing Ruse to walk backward ahead of her, all of them getting closer to the Performer—and the end of the belt.

Without knowing what else to do, Ruse enfolds Mim in her arms. Feast follows suit, the two of them doing their best to shield the smaller girl from the Performer.

Mim stops walking. She sniffles.

Ruse pulls away and sees the girl crying. Her tears track down the white paint, washing it from her face.

"Okay?" Ruse asks.

Mim nods. Then she looks past her and her eyes widen.

Feast leans close to her ear and whispers something. Ruse doesn't hear and she can't read his lips behind his mask, but what he says isn't for her anyway. Then he takes Mim's left hand gently.

Ruse stands on her right side and slips her hand into Mim's. The three of them confront the Performer, who stands frozen on the moving conveyor belt, arms spread out at his sides, grasping for hands that aren't there. Blurred black lines run down his white face, as though his eyes are melting. Behind him, the remains of his crate and the broken door to his room tumble off the end of the belt, down into nothing but the open sky.

Mim bows to him, still holding on to Feast and Ruse's hands. At the same time, the Performer bows. His beret falls from his head onto the belt between them, and a moment later, he goes over the edge too.

An anguished cry shatters the silence, fading into the clouds below.

The Performer had a voice after all.

# CHAPTER 10

**The three kids look at one another as the** Performer's scream slowly fades. The conveyor belt continues to carry them forward. Feast glances behind them at the loading dock, but as Ruse considers the Giant Wheel turning in the distance, she has a revelation: There is no going back. Not back to the carnival, not back to their old lives.

She shakes her head. Feast frowns uncertainly, but he shrugs. Ruse squeezes his and Mim's hands.

Ruse has always wanted to feel like she belongs. She

just didn't know until now that it wasn't a *place* she yearned for. While her memories remain unclear, she wonders if that's why she jumped that night. But it doesn't matter anymore why. What matters is that it brought her to Feast and Mim.

They've seen a balloon ship come and go. Those cargo crates are waiting to be transported off the flying carnival. There's much more to this place, wherever and whatever it is—and for better or worse, the three of them are part of it now. It has been affecting them, but they are affecting *it* too, as well as one another. She is different after meeting Mim and Feast, but she also has never been more herself.

*I am Ruse*, she thinks.

But perhaps not all change has been for the better. Feast is wasting away before her. He urgently needs food and rest.

And Mim . . . she seems like a new person, almost unrecognizable from before. She stands straight, with none of her usual shy nervousness. Is she truly free of the Performer's influence? Rub as she might, Mim's face paint won't come off. She catches Ruse studying her and some emotion flashes over her eyes, too quick to register, before she smiles and nods.

*I'll have to watch her more closely*, Ruse thinks, feeling guilty about her suspicion.

It's possible that nowhere is truly safe for them, but that won't keep them from looking. Still linked hand in hand, Ruse leads the others to the Performer's dropped beret. She picks it up and several black apples fall out and then roll off the conveyor belt.

Ruse grabs onto the brim, and Feast and Mim take hold of it at two other points, their positions forming a triangle. They pull on it and the beret begins to stretch, wider and wider.

They don't wait for the conveyor belt to launch them off the airship. They stride forward in perfect unison, and they *jump*.

Ruse's stomach drops and she feels a rush of adrenaline, like on the carnival roller coaster. But as they fall, the beret gradually fills with air. It balloons above them, slowing their descent. Clouds swirl and wisp around them as they gently drift with no sense of direction or movement.

She recalls sinking, being pushed down into dark, watery depths. Now she feels weightless, like floating in a dream. In the soft focus of her surroundings, her thoughts scatter and wander. More lost memories bubble to the surface of her mind. Her consciousness begins to slip . . .

She catches herself before her fingers let go of the beret and tightens her grip. Jolted back to awareness, she checks on the others.

Feast's gaze is downcast, searching for whatever might lie below. Meanwhile, Mim's eyes are glassily fixed on the ship above as if she has left behind something important up there.

Ruse has never been able to consider the future, and she isn't certain they can even make one here. So it's best to concentrate on surviving in the now. Suspended in this tenuous moment, she shifts her attention toward the far horizon, anticipation and apprehension meeting where sky touches sea.

END

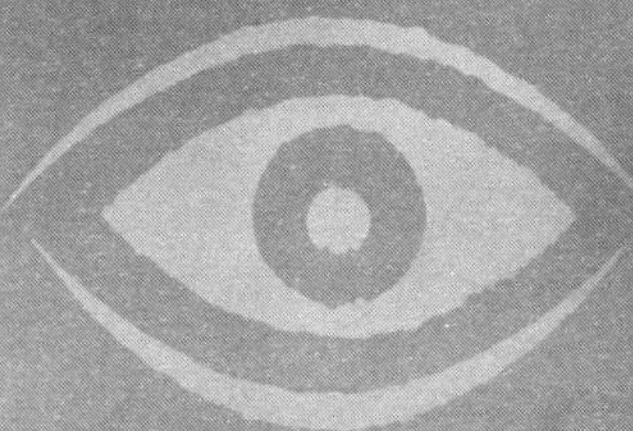

# ABOUT THE AUTHOR

**E. C. Myers was assembled in the U.S. from** Korean and German parts and raised by a single mother and the public library in Yonkers, New York. He is the author of numerous short stories and four young adult books: the Andre Norton Award–winning *Fair Coin*, *Quantum Coin*, *The Silence of Six*, and *Against All Silence*. E. C. currently lives with his wife, son, and three doofy pets in Pennsylvania. You can find traces of him all over the internet, but especially at ecmyers.net and on X: @ecmyers.